Thrilling T̶ ̶ ̶ ̶ ̶ ̶ ̶ ̶ ̶ ̶ ̶ of

Suspense and Science Fiction

By David Caglarcan

Thrilling Tales: Short Stories of Suspense and Science Fiction

Copyright © 2021 David A. Caglarcan

Acknowledgments

I am especially grateful to my wife, my parents, my brother, and my sister-in-law for their loving support, including their willingness to read rough drafts and provide helpful feedback. I am also grateful to Pablo Del Rio for his timely assistance in editing the final draft, and to Victor Arellano for his valuable contribution to the production of the cover art. In addition, I owe thanks to several of my elementary, middle, and high school teachers, who, decades ago, planted in me the idea that I could be a writer. Most of all, I am grateful to my extraordinary son, whose strength and courage inspire me daily.

Table of Contents

Mom's Crystal

I stood at the edge of Signal Knob Scenic Overlook in Virginia's Shenandoah National Park and surveyed the vast expanse of the Shenandoah Valley. It was a cloudless, mild, March afternoon. Patches of brilliant green punctuated the predominantly brown and yellow landscape below us, portending the onset of Spring. In the distance, the Blue Ridge Mountains loomed beneath a sun-drenched sky.

"Beautiful, isn't it?" my wife Susan said, gently squeezing my left hand. "Thanks so much for agreeing to come here today. I know it's a long drive. But isn't it worth it, just for the view?"

"Anything for you, sweetie," I replied. "And yes, it is worth it."

On my right side, I held the hand of our eleven-year-old son, Jake. This was his first trip to see the famous mountain views on Skyline Drive. "What do you think, Jake? Quite a view, eh?"

Jake turned and looked at me, his face intense. "Where's Mom? I want Mom."

"Well, of course, Jake, she's right—" I realized that Susan's hand was no longer in mine. I turned to my left. She was gone. "Wait. She was just here. Susan?"

"I want Mom," Jake repeated. "Where did she go? Where did she go?"

"Susan, where are you?" I repeated. "Susan!"

"I want Mom. I want Mom! Dad, where is she?" Jake's grip on my hand tightened.

"Susan," I said, "where are you? Susan, come back!"

I snapped awake. Jake stood by my bed, both of his hands gripping my right hand. In the faint glow from the alarm clock on the night table, I could see tears streaming down his cheeks.

"Where is she, Dad? What happened to Mom?"

I reached out to the left side of the bed—the side where Susan slept—and felt the empty mattress. She'd been gone a mere two days. Our trip to Skyline Drive, of which I'd dreamed, had taken place the previous weekend. "Oh, Jake," I said, "I'm so sorry, son. We talked about this today, remember? Mom went to heaven."

"Where's Mom? Where's Mom?"

"Jake, listen—"

"I want Mom! Where is she?"

Any young boy would find the loss of his mother impossible to accept. For Jake, afflicted with autism, the loss was unfathomable. Had the man who'd killed Susan—the idiot who thought he could drive after chugging an entire six-pack of beer—realized the devastation he would cause, he might have reconsidered his actions. "Oh, Jake," I said. "We're going to get through this, I promise." At that moment, I wasn't sure I believed my own words. "It's going to be okay."

I felt an explosion on the side of my head and realized that Jake had struck me. In the dim light, I hadn't seen the blow coming. Before I could react, he hit me again, his hand thudding against my nose and delivering a jolt of pain that watered my eyes.

It had been months since Jake's last violent meltdown; this was an area in which he'd made tremendous progress over the years. But the shock of losing his mother had unleashed the worst demons of his autism. "No, Jake!" I reached out to grab him, but he kept flailing.

For a few seconds, we struggled. I managed to get Jake into a bear hug, and I held on. Finally, after a minute or so, he collapsed into my arms—sweaty, spent, and sobbing. After sliding him onto Susan's side of the bed, I whispered comforting words into his ear as he drifted off to sleep. I rolled over onto my side of the bed and stared into the abyss, wanting to cry but somehow unable to. Lord God, I thought, why have you done this? How could you take her from us?

I don't know how we managed to survive the next few days. My family was wonderful. They handled the funeral arrangements on my behalf, allowing me to focus on Jake. As a result, things went relatively smoothly, and Jake managed to stay calm through the entire ordeal.

In the weeks that followed, the impact of Susan's death became painfully apparent. Jake grew depressed and withdrawn, seldom willing to leave his bedroom. At school, he remained a socially awkward loner, as he'd always been. The precious few friendships that he'd fostered during happier times—a development largely facilitated by Susan—faded away. I suspect the other kids must've found him unapproachable in his grief-stricken state. I even worried about the possibility of Jake being bullied. Fortunately, this did not come to pass.

Such was our life during those bleak days of March 2015. Though I'd arranged to telecommute for my job and could therefore devote more time to Jake, I was unable to lift his spirits. I couldn't cajole him into taking a drive to the mall or his favorite restaurant, Panera Bread. I had to pester him mercilessly to do his homework; we often engaged in a battle of wills that dragged late into the evening, concluding with my giving in to his demand for ice cream or some other treat. Now and then, the demons of autism rose up again, and Jake became dysregulated. Fortunately, he always managed to calm down; things never got out of control.

As the nights of insufficient sleep piled up, and Jake's progress toward emotional stability continued at a frustratingly slow pace, a sense of darkness set in. I often dulled my pain with a late-night cocktail. I prayed daily, but it felt as though God were a universe away.

The advent of April brought warmer weather and a slight bit of hope that things might improve. I had a notion that we were finally going to catch a break; something significant and positive would happen. I knew not the source of my premonition. In fact, I tried not to dwell on it, lest I set myself up for a disappointment.

"Wow, that's cool," Jake said. We were seated at the dining room table, Jake's science homework spread out before us. We had just read a summary of Newton's Third Law of Motion, which states that for every action, there is an equal and opposite reaction. The text explained how this principle is exemplified in rocket propulsion. During launch, the burning fuel exerts a downward force, and the reaction force pushes against the rocket, causing it to climb. "That's how the space shuttle worked, right Dad?"

"Uh, yeah," I replied. I was taken aback by Jake's rather abrupt expression of interest, given his usual lethargy when it came to homework and studying. "The space shuttle, the Saturn Five moon rocket, the Soyuz, the SpaceX Falcon Nine...all rockets use this principle."

For nearly an hour, we discussed science, rocketry, and the space program—topics that had fascinated me since childhood. To my delight, these topics apparently interested Jake, as well. It was the liveliest conversation we'd had in weeks. By the time we retired for the night, having completed Jake's homework, an idea had formed in my mind.

The following Saturday afternoon, we stood on the 50-yard line of one of the well-manicured soccer fields at Morgan's Grove Park in Shepherdstown, West Virginia, beneath a partly cloudy sky. Before us, on a small, tripod launch pad, stood an 18-inch-tall model rocket, constructed from cardboard, balsa wood, and plastic. A thin coat of glossy white spray paint gave the craft a flashy veneer, and its name, the "Starlifter," was inscribed on its fuselage in bold black font. Installed in the bottom of the rocket was an "A8-3" engine—a three-inch long paper tube containing tightly packed gunpowder that, in proper conditions, could be expected to lift the vehicle 400 feet into the sky. Protruding from the engine were two ignition wires, to which were attached a fifteen-foot cable that led to the launch control device I held in my hand.

Inspired by Jake's fascination with Newton's Third Law and its application to rocketry and spaceflight, I'd purchased the rocket kit online earlier that week. The day it arrived, I stayed up most of the night assembling it.

"You see, Jake," I said, "when we attach the safety key to the controller, it will arm the system. Then, when we push the ignition button, a 6-volt electrical current will pass through the wires all the way to the igniter, which is attached to the engine. The igniter will emit a flame, igniting the engine, causing liftoff. Pretty cool, eh?"

"Yeah," Jake murmured. "Sounds good, Dad." I couldn't tell if Jake's enthusiasm for rocketry had diminished over the past several days, or if he merely found our miniature spaceship unimpressive compared to the space shuttles and other rockets we'd discussed.

Whatever the case, I hoped that he'd change his outlook when he saw the rocket actually fly.

"You know, this is the first time you and I have been out together, just to do something fun, in a long time," I said. "I really think you're going to like this. A true demonstration of Newton's laws, in our own little rocket."

"Sure, Dad. Can we just launch it?"

"Okay, okay. Here you go. I've inserted the safety key, and I'm handing you the controller. When I count down to zero, you press the launch button down and hold it down. Ready: five... four... three... two... one... zero!"

Jake pressed the launch button. We waited in silence. In the distance, a bird chirped. "Dad," Jake said, "Nothing's happen—"

With a thunderous "whoosh," the Starlifter leaped skyward, leaving behind a cloud of smoke and the smell of gunpowder. Within a second, the rocket was at least 200 feet in the air and climbing fast. I squinted as I watched it coast to the top of its flight path, at least 400 feet up. A couple seconds later, the engine's "ejection charge" fired, separating the nose cone from the fuselage and deploying the parachute. Less than ten seconds after liftoff, the craft was floating gently earthward.

"Wow! Wow!" Jake's eyes were wide like saucers as he looked skyward at the descending rocket. "Dad, that was awesome!"

"You liked it?"

"It was amazing!" For the first time in months, Jake smiled—a broad, irresistible grin.

As I watched the rocket touch down on the turf, about fifty yards away from us, I said a silent prayer of gratitude.

"Come on, Dad, let's go get it!" Jake took off running toward the rocket.

For our second flight, I let Jake do all the preparations—extracting the spent engine from the rocket and inserting a fresh one, placing flame-resistant "recovery wadding" inside the rocket and re-packing the parachute, positioning the rocket on the launch pad, and connecting the ignition wires. We loaded the rocket with a "B" engine, theoretically twice as powerful as the "A" engine we'd used for the initial flight.

Jake performed the verbal countdown, pushing the ignition button at "zero." This time, propelled by the stronger engine, the Starlifter flew so high that we lost sight of it. Fortunately, I'd brought a set of binoculars, and I sighted the rocket as it coasted across the sky, just prior to the deployment of the parachute. "There it is, Jake! Take a look!" I handed him the binoculars. "The parachute is about to deploy."

"I see it," he said. "Chute looks good, and it's coming down nicely."

We conducted two more launches with "B" engines, both of which went flawlessly. Then, noticing that it was almost dinner time, I said, "Okay, Jake, we've got time for one more. We can use another 'B' engine, or we can use a 'C' engine, which is even more powerful. What do you think?"

"Let's use the 'C' engine."

"I've got to warn you: the C engine is very powerful. When I used 'C' engines in my rockets when I was a kid, I'd end up losing the rocket about a third of the time. They'd fly so high that I'd lose track of them. So, if we launch with a 'C' engine, there's a chance we'll lose the Starlifter. You need to be okay with that."

"If we lose it, can we build another rocket?"

"You bet. In fact, we can have one ready to fly by next weekend."

"Then let's do it, Dad!"

As we prepared the Starlifter for its final flight of the day, Jake noticed something he hadn't seen earlier. "What's this?" he asked, pointing to the small, hollow section of the rocket just aft of the nose cone.

"Ah yes, the payload section." I explained to Jake that, like many model rockets, the Starlifter had a small cargo compartment to allow for the launching of small objects—for example, keepsakes, tiny electronic devices, even insects.

"Can we put something in there now?"

"Sure. Did you have something in mind?"

"How about a bug?"

"Sure, I suppose, if you can find one."

Within a minute, Jake had produced a small grasshopper, which he gingerly deposited into the cargo section of the rocket. "This should work, right Dad?"

"Sure. But let's make a deal. As soon as the rocket lands, we let the grasshopper go. If we forget about it and leave it inside the rocket, it'll die. Okay?"

Jake agreed to my terms, and we proceeded with the launch preparations. But as we went about our work, I started having second thoughts about the grasshopper. What if the rocket crashed? That was unlikely, but possible. What if we lost the rocket? The grasshopper may remain trapped inside and suffocate. Maybe this grasshopper thing wasn't such a good idea, I thought.

Suddenly and inexplicably, my concerns evaporated—replaced by an odd, reassuring feeling that we were, indeed, doing the right thing. Yes, we must proceed with the launch, using the "C" engine, with the grasshopper on board.

When the rocket was ready, Jake handed me the launch controller and grabbed the binoculars. "You push the button this time, Dad. I'll track the rocket."

After Jake counted down to zero, I pushed the button, and the rocket blasted skyward until it was well beyond the view of the naked eye, achieving an altitude of at least 1000 feet. When the main engine burn completed and the rocket started its coast toward apogee, Jake scanned the sky with the binoculars.

"Any luck, Jake? Do you see it?"

"Nope, not yet. Oh wait…no, I still can't see it."

We continued searching the sky for another thirty seconds or so, to no avail. "Well, Jake," I said, "it must've drifted somewhere beyond the park. I'm sorry, son. We knew this might happen. Poor grasshopper."

"Wait, Dad I think…I see it! There it is!" To my astonishment, the Starlifter appeared, almost directly overhead, gently descending beneath its parachute. It settled onto the ground a mere twenty yards from the launch pad.

"Amazing," I said. "I've never seen a rocket fly so high and then land so close to the launch pad."

Jake picked up the rocket from the grass. "Well," he said, "I guess that's our final flight. Time to pack up and get going, right?"

"Yes, but aren't you forgetting something?"

"Oh, of course!" Jake knelt down, removed the nose cone from the rocket, and tilted the cargo section downward so that the grasshopper would have a gentle landing. We waited...and waited some more...and nothing came out of the rocket. "Where is it?" Jake asked. He lifted the cargo section up to his face and looked in. "I don't see it, Dad!"

"Let me see. Maybe it's just way in the back. Maybe the G forces were too much. Oh man, I hope we didn't crush the poor thing!" I examined the payload compartment, but there was no sign of the grasshopper. I tilted it downward and shook it—rather a senseless action, given that we'd already verified that our insect astronaut was gone.

Then, the oddest thing happened. A white, spherical rock, about half an inch in diameter, fell out of the cargo section onto the grass. I picked it up. "What's this?" I asked. "Jake, did you put this in there?"

19

Jake shook his head, and he looked as puzzled as I felt. "I just put a grasshopper, Dad. That's all."

"Well, our grasshopper is gone, and instead, we've got this little item." I studied the rock and quickly realized that it wasn't like any rock I'd ever seen. From a distance of one foot, it appeared to be an ordinary white stone—albeit almost perfectly spherical. But when I held it close to my eyes, its outer surface became transparent, and I could see about a dozen tiny crystals inside, each one as brilliant as a diamond. "Jake, we've really got something here! Have a look."

I handed it to Jake, and he examined it. "Wow," he whispered.

"Hold it close to your eyes. See the crystals inside?"

"I see them. Amazing!" He looked some more, and then handed it back to me. "But Dad, where did it come from? How did it get into the rocket? And what happened to the grasshopper?"

"I don't know, son, I really don't. But...there's got to be an explanation."

20

"Maybe the rock was inside the rocket all along," Jake said, "and we just didn't notice it. Maybe it was inside the cargo section when you built the rocket, and you somehow didn't see it."

"Well," I replied, "I suppose that's possible. But that still doesn't explain what happened to the grasshopper. How did it just disappear like that?" For several seconds, we stood in bemused silence.

"Dad," Jake said, "you know how you said I should tell you whenever I feel my anxiety getting bad?"

"Yes."

"It's starting to get bad."

"Don't worry, son," I said, putting my arm around his shoulder. "Everything is fine. We just have a bit of a mystery on our hands--that's all." Beneath my hand, I felt Jake's body starting to shake. The inexplicable events of the past few minutes had disrupted his autistic sense of order, his need for predictability. "It's all good, Jake. Really, it's all good."

"We need to figure this out, Dad." His voice started to crack. "There has to be an explanation! We've got to—"

A pulse of warm sunlight hit my face. Apparently, the sun had crept out from behind a cloud. Then, I noticed something quite peculiar. Jake had stopped shaking. "Feeling better, son?"

"Yeah," he replied, his voice noticeably calmer. "I do feel better. I don't know why, but I'm not nervous anymore. It's okay if we don't understand what happened. It's okay." Having been on the verge of a tearful meltdown just moments before, he appeared relaxed.

"You know, you're absolutely right," I replied. "Come here, boy!" I pulled him into a tight embrace and held him close for a few seconds. It felt like a little bit of Heaven.

We packed up our gear, working mostly in silence, each of us immersed in his own thoughts about the events of the day. Try as I might, I couldn't conjure an explanation for the disappearance of the grasshopper and the arrival of the mysterious rock. Nor could I fathom how a random burst of sunlight had calmed Jake's anxiety and left him so thoroughly content. Susan had always believed in divine intervention—the notion of a loving God who acts in the world on behalf of human beings. I'd never been able to accept the idea. But now, as Jake and I climbed into the car, I couldn't help but wonder.

We went to Panera Bread for dinner. Jake ordered his old favorite, the chicken panini sandwich. As we sat at a window-side table and enjoyed our meal, I reveled in his cheerful disposition. "You've got the crystal with you, right?" I asked.

"Right," he replied. "I've got it in my right pocket."

"Good. Until we get home, you keep a close eye on it. Then, we'll find a really nice spot for it in your bedroom. Okay?"

"Okay."

In between bites of his sandwich, Jake looked me in the eyes. "I think I've figured it out, Dad."

"Figured out what?"

"Where the crystal came from."

"Really? Where?"

He paused for a moment, and then said quietly, "It came from Heaven. Mom sent it."

Taken aback, I sat silently. I felt an urge to say something like, 'that's a beautiful thought, but there must be a rational explanation.' But I had no such explanation, and I couldn't rule out the possibility that something supernatural had, indeed, taken place. If Jake believed that his mother was helping us from Heaven, I had no good reason to discourage such a belief. Normally so disposed toward a logical, even rigid pattern of thinking, my son was demonstrating a capacity for faith that was far greater than my own. "Well, Jake," I said, "you may be right."

"Of course I'm right." He took the crystal out of his pocket and set it on the table. "From now on, we will call it Mom's Crystal. Whenever we miss Mom, we can look at this crystal and we'll know she's watching over us from Heaven. What do you think, Dad?"

I wasn't ready for the surge of emotion that hit me. Many times, over the course of the past several weeks, I'd wanted to cry, but the tears never came.

24

Now, they burst forth in a torrent. I buried my face in my hands and felt a salty sting in my eyes.

"You okay, Dad?"

I nodded, trying to regain my composure. I must've been quite a sight. Finally, my tears subsided, and I wiped my face with a napkin. "Son," I said in a thick voice, "I love your idea. Today, we were given Mom's Crystal. We'll always cherish it. It'll remind us that Mom is always with us."

As we drove home beneath a moonlit sky, I wondered what the future held. If we had, indeed, experienced a miracle, would our lives be different now? Had the darkness finally been lifted?

Before we retired to bed that night, we placed Mom's Crystal inside an antique jewelry box that Susan had received as a gift from her grandmother. It had been one of her most prized possessions, and thus, it seemed an appropriate place to put the crystal. We placed the jewelry box on top of Jake's bedroom dresser, next to a framed picture of Susan.

We said our prayers, including a prayer of thanks to God for the gift of Mom's Crystal, and I kissed Jake on the forehead. "I love you, son."

"I love you too, Dad."

When I checked on him twenty minutes later, he was asleep.

The following several weeks gave proof that we had, indeed, turned a corner. Though he was not immune from bouts of sadness and dysregulation, Jake's overall mood was vastly improved. He was more productive in school and he was getting along better with his classmates. He tackled his homework willingly—even enthusiastically when it came to math and science. By the time the school year ended in June, his grades had fully recovered to the superlative level that he'd achieved prior to Susan's passing.

We continued launching rockets on the weekends. In addition, we did other fun things together, such as going to movies, arcades, and theme parks. Jake read books about space—biographies of famous astronauts, histories of the space program, and even "Interplanetary Flight," the legendary Arthur C. Clarke's introduction to the science of space travel. We watched several of the classic space films, such as "2001: A Space Odyssey," "The Right Stuff," "Apollo 13," and "Interstellar."

That summer, we vacationed in Orlando, Florida. The highlight of our trip was our daylong visit to the Kennedy Space Center at Cape Canaveral. We were awestruck by the massive Saturn Five moon rocket, the 3-D virtual Mars landscape, and the Atlantis space shuttle. We felt giddy as we climbed aboard the shuttle launch simulator, and we laughed with joy as our cheeks flapped against our jaws from the powerful rumble of the simulated rocket engines.

We drove back to our hotel beneath an orange and violet sunset that reflected beautifully off the surface of the Banana River. "You know, Dad," said Jake, "I want to work for NASA when I grow up."

"Sounds great," I replied. "Do you want to be an astronaut?"

"No, I think I might have trouble with the crazy training they do. Too much disruption to my routines. I'd rather be one of the engineers in Mission Control.

I'd like to design rockets and spacecraft. I want to help us get to Mars."

"You can do it, son. It'll take a lot of studying and hard work, but I'm sure you can make it happen. And I'll help you any way that I can."

******

More than two decades later, during the momentous summer of 2038, Jake's dream was realized when the international Mars One crew landed in the deep canyon of Valles Marineris along the Martian equator. As the astronauts expertly set their craft down upon the surface of the red planet, Jake manned the "Guidance Officer" station in Mission Control at the Johnson Space Center in Houston, Texas. By now an accomplished aerospace engineer and computer programmer with a master's degree from Virginia Tech, Jake had played a key role in monitoring the performance of the spacecraft's guidance systems throughout its months-long interplanetary journey.

Watching news coverage of the mission on TV from my townhouse in the Houston suburbs (like Jake, I had relocated to the area several years earlier), I thought about that day in April 2015 when Jake and I launched our first rocket and Mom's Crystal entered our lives. The ensuing years had provided us with adventures and challenges, triumphs and setbacks. Jake had slogged his way through middle school and high school, excelling in academics while struggling with the social aspect of school. Dismissed by the "cool kids" as a nerd, often rejected by girls due to his awkward demeanor, he still managed to maintain a small group of friends who shared his interests. At Virginia Tech, he found a group of kindred spirits in the engineering school—fellow nerds with over-sized intellects and lofty goals. He stayed for six years, earning his master's degree in aerospace engineering.

By the time Jake became a NASA mission controller in Houston, he'd made tremendous progress in his journey with autism. He had his own apartment and a great circle of friends—mostly co-workers from the Johnson Space Center. His idealistic enthusiasm for the space program inspired others and drew people to him. His anxiety, though quite strong at times, never controlled him. He took his medications and carefully monitored his health.

Jake even had a fiancée—a brilliant, blue-eyed NASA geologist. Lovely, patient, and kind, Dana seemed the perfect soulmate for Jake. In many ways, she reminded me of Susan.

All through the years, Jake's most treasured possession, Mom's Crystal, had remained on his bedroom dresser. Each night before bed, he'd take it out of its box and hold it in his hand as he said his prayers.

******

Dressed in white smocks, cloth hats, surgical masks, and gloves, the three of us—Jake, Dana, and I—stepped into a bland, antiseptic room within the Extraterrestrial Receiving Laboratory (ERL) at the Johnson Space Center. The ERL is the facility where rock and soil samples from Mars and other planetary bodies are stored and studied. Some of the world's most renowned geologists work there. The Mars One crew even lived within the ERL during their one-month quarantine period after returning to Earth.

I gazed upon what looked like an enormous steel refrigerator with a clear glass front—the type you see in the frozen food section of a grocery store. But this was no refrigerator; it was a sophisticated, vacuum-sealed container designed for the study of extraterrestrial samples. Several "manipulation stations" were affixed, side-by-side, to the glass. Each of these stations contained an "arm and glove assembly"—a pair of coiled rubber tubes that extended into the container, each of which ended in a sturdy, nylon-lined glove. By inserting their arms into the tubes, the geologists could handle the Martian samples without contaminating them. Inside the container, tethered to each shelf, were sets of metallic tongs to assist the geologists in manipulating the samples.

On the shelves, beneath florescent lights, sat dozens of samples of Mars—magnificent, rugged, rust-colored rocks of various shapes and sizes.

"We're pretty lucky that I married a NASA geologist," said Jake, referring to the fact that Dana's position as a key geologist within the ERL had netted us our VIP access. (Their wedding had taken place a few weeks earlier).

"This is amazing," I said. "We're looking at pieces of another planet. I can hardly believe it!" I thanked Dana profusely. I wanted to hug her, but it seemed inappropriate in such a clinical setting.

"Dad," Jake said, "there's a particular set of samples I want to show you. I noticed them when Dana showed me around the other day. As soon as I saw them, I thought of you."

"Sure, let's have a look!"

I followed Jake as he walked to the left side of the room, stopping in front of the left-most portion of the steel container. "Look, Dad. Check out the ones on the top shelf."

"Well, they look just like the others. I don't see any diff—"

Then, I saw them. Among the rough Martian rocks were several samples that were quite different

32

indeed—smooth, white objects, about the size of your palm, and nearly perfectly spherical. I put my face closer to the glass.

"Do those remind you of something?" Jake asked.

"I...I don't believe it. Are those...can we use the manipulation station to get a closer view?"

"I'm afraid you can't," said Dana, "but I can."

Moments later, Dana held one of the spherical objects in her gloved hand, just inside the glass barrier, only an inch from my eyes. As I looked closely, I saw dozens of tiny crystals, perfectly formed, brilliant like diamonds, contained within the sphere.

"Jake," I said, dumbfounded. "Jake...how—"

"Maybe I can explain," said Dana. "These samples were found a few inches underground, about ten yards away from the spacecraft. They were among the first samples collected by the astronauts. They didn't look like this on the surface, though. They were encased within larger rocks that looked just like all the others. The spheres appeared later, here in the lab, when we broke up the larger samples. It really baffled us. Have you noticed there's been nothing in the press about these samples? NASA's keeping this quiet, at least until we can figure out what the heck these things are. In fact, I'm really surprised I was able to get you guys in here."

"Jake," I said, "Does Dana know...about...."

"Yes, Dad, of course she knows. She's my wife! As soon as she saw these samples, she thought of Mom's Crystal. And as soon as I saw them, I agreed the resemblance was obvious."

"These samples seem to have the exact same shape and appearance as Mom's Crystal, but they're significantly larger," I said.

"I concur," said Jake. "Mom's Crystal is basically a miniature version of these samples—just small enough to fit in the payload section of a kid's model rocket."

"Remember when we went out to eat that evening, after we found Mom's Crystal, and you said it was a miracle? Jake, I think we've just encountered miracle number two."

That evening, the three of us enjoyed a quiet dinner at Jake and Dana's apartment. I often dined with them—a welcome change from my solitary, though pleasant, existence.

"So, Dad," Jake said as we devoured our panini sandwiches, "I'd like to get your thoughts on what we saw today—your deep thoughts, I mean. We know what we saw, but what's the significance of it?"

"Well," I replied, "I'm still in shock. As I said before, I think it's a miracle. But now that I've had some time to reflect on it, I've got an idea—a theory of how those Martian samples fit into the grand scheme of your life.

"You see, your mother had big dreams for you. She knew you could do extraordinary things, in spite of your autism. When she was taken from us so suddenly, it was a terrible blow—not just for us, but for her, too. She watched us from above, and it broke her heart to see you suffer. She needed to find a way to inspire you. So, she sent us a miracle, in the form of a strange crystal in the cargo section of our model rocket. It worked. You were inspired, and so was I.

"All these years you've studied and worked and struggled, you knew your mother was watching over you, sending her love. And she knew that you'd succeed. She knew you'd play a role in the exploration of Mars. She had to have known; why else would she have put a tiny piece of Mars into our little model rocket?

"And that's it—that's my explanation. What do you two think?"

I noticed both Jake and Dana's faces were wet with streaming tears. Then, I realized that I, too, was crying.

"I think you nailed it, Dad," Jake said, softly.

******

Several months have passed since I visited the ERL with Jake and Dana and beheld the crystalline Martian samples. The existence of these remarkable specimens has since been publicized, fueling an even greater level of public interest in the red planet—not to mention a host of crackpot conspiracy theories about aliens, government cover-ups, and the like.

Yet one authentic conspiracy does, indeed, exist—well beyond the wildest speculations of the internet trolls. I refer, of course, to the conspiracy of silence between myself, Jake, and Dana regarding Mom's Crystal. The way the crystal appeared inside a kid's model rocket more than twenty years before mankind's arrival on Mars was indeed a miracle, one that defies any rational explanation. Thus, rather than try to explain it, we've chosen to simply be grateful for it—and, to keep it as our family secret.

What a joy it's been to watch Jake and Dana strengthen their bonds of love and mutual respect during this first year of their marriage. All Jake's years of effort and striving have been richly rewarded. In spite of all the challenges he's faced, he's managed to achieve that rare combination of personal and professional success that eludes most people.

I gaze upon Mom's Crystal, which sits on my nightstand. Jake brought it over about three weeks ago, the day I received my cancer diagnosis. I felt awkward accepting it, given that it's been by Jake's side these many years, but he insisted. Now, as I study the treasured item, which sits next to a framed picture of Susan, I'm grateful to have it.

Stage Four cancer is often insurmountable, and I know my odds aren't great. My recovery from the initial surgery and radiation treatment was painful, and the subsequent chemotherapy has left me exhausted most of the time. Fortunately, my home-care nursing robot meets all my daily needs and keeps my townhouse in good order, and a very kind human nurse drops by each morning to check on me. Most evenings, Jake and Dana stop by as well. Some nights, I sleep well. Some nights, I don't.

In spite of the physical discomfort that characterizes my existence, I'm content. I've lived a full life, and I've even managed to make a small contribution to the world in the form of my son. In the coming years, Jake and Dana will continue their important work in the space program. In addition, I suspect they'll start a family of their own before long.

I'm confident that somehow, I'll overcome this cancer. And yet, whether I live just one more hour or twenty more years, my life is already complete. I'm grateful for the many blessings I've been given.

Exhaustion bears heavily upon me. I whisper a quick prayer and turn off the light on my nightstand. My head sinks into the pillow, and the velvety darkness of night surrounds me.

I stand at the edge of Signal Knob Overlook in Virginia's Shenandoah National Park and survey the vast expanse of the Shenandoah Valley. It is a partly cloudy, mild, March afternoon.

"Beautiful, isn't it?" Susan says.

I feel her warm hand in mine and give it a gentle squeeze. "Beautiful, indeed," I reply.

"Come over here. I want to show you something." She tugs at my hand.

"Wait—let me check on Jake first. Have you seen him?" I scan the area and find Jake's car, parked about twenty yards away at the entrance of the overlook. He's standing outside the car with Dana. They're enjoying a tender moment; their love for one another is clearly apparent.

"Don't worry about Jake," Susan says. "He's fine."

I realize we've traversed several yards from our original spot, though I don't recall moving my feet. "Wait," I protest. "I can't just leave Jake without saying something."

"Look at how happy he is with Dana. What an amazing love they share. He's in such good hands. And besides, you're not leaving him. Did I ever leave you?" I feel Susan's lips gently kissing my cheek, her warm breath against my skin.

"No, you never did."

"You'll always be with Jake, no matter what happens. And so will I."

Somehow, we've traversed off the edge of the overlook and we're suspended in mid-air, literally floating above the scene. Jake and Dana have walked to the spot where Susan I stood just moments before. They hold hands and talk quietly as they marvel at the panorama beneath them.

The sunlight reflects off Susan's long, blonde locks. She's as young and vibrant as the last time I saw

40

her. Then, I look down and realize that we've ascended at least a hundred feet into the air. Jake and Dana remain visible, but they grow smaller with each passing second.

"Susan, what's going on? What—"

"Don't worry, darling," she says. "It'll all make sense in just a minute or so."

I start to realize what's happening. "Susan, are you sure it's okay to leave Jake? I don't feel right about this."

"My love, don't worry. As I said before, you aren't really leaving him. As long as he has the crystal, he has both of us. And Dana will never leave his side."

White vapor surrounds us, and I realize we're passing through a cloud deck. Once we're above the puffs of mist, I look down again. Through a gap in the clouds, I can see the scenic overlook, and I can just pick out Jake and Dana. They're so small—barely distinguishable from the surrounding scenery. Our rate of climb is increasing.

"Susan, are we really...I mean, am I...."

"We'll never be apart again."

Now, I can see the horizon, scores of miles away. The clouds through which we passed, only moments before, are far below. The sky starts to darken, and the curvature of the Earth becomes apparent. "Susan, this is extraordinary."

"This is nothing, my love, compared to the wonders that await us."

Seconds later, we are miles high and still climbing, and yet I feel as warm and comfortable as I did when I stood on the overlook. Susan gives my hand another squeeze, and I start to allow myself to believe that this is real. I ponder the years I've spent without her—all the lonely nights that I've longed for her touch. I imagine what it will be like to hold her again.

We climb even higher, to the edge of space, and I marvel at the expanse of North America beneath us. Then, almost instantly, the Earth itself seems to be receding, as our rate of climb accelerates even more. I catch a glimpse of the Aurora Borealis, its green fluorescence floating above the Arctic Circle, and then it, too, falls away. Nearly the entire face of the Earth is visible—a fragile, beautiful blue marble whose very existence testifies to the unimaginable glory of God. In the distance, thousands of stars punctuate the gentle blackness.

"Look up, my love," Susan whispers.

Looking upward, I behold a light that is even more brilliant than the Sun itself, and yet somehow bearable to my eyes. We're climbing steadily into this light. Further up, I can discern the faint silhouettes of countless souls.

"My love," she says, "you're coming home."

The silhouettes grow larger and more numerous as we continue to ascend. The Earth and the blackness of space are no longer visible; we are enveloped by light.

I turn to her, squeezing her hand. "You know, sweetheart," I say, "there's something I've really been wanting to ask you for many years."

"Of course. What is it, love?"

"What, exactly, did happen to that grasshopper?"

The Epochal Objective

Drone 6745 Status Report, 21:34:30 Universal Coordinated Time. Location: 40.83 North, 109.68 East. Altitude: 10,668 meters. Velocity: 550 knots. Heading: 234 degrees true. Target downrange distance: 28.35 nautical miles. Internal systems status: nominal. Fuel level: 74.66 percent. Telemetry data attached. Awaiting authorization for weapon release. Drone 6745 concludes.

"Global Command Authority acknowledges." Septimus 78 stood at the command console and processed the status report, which had just arrived via Top Secret data link from the skies over Inner Mongolia, China. Reviewing the telemetry data from the drone, he confirmed that the aircraft's status was, indeed, nominal.

As required in any operation involving nuclear weapons, Septimus 78 initiated an additional processing thread to perform a final—albeit redundant—assessment of the mission's moral implications. After 36.7 milliseconds, the review was complete, the conclusion obvious: the criticality of this mission outweighed all humanitarian consequences. He relayed his authorization message via the data link, simultaneously speaking it aloud for the benefit of those robots who were not linked in. "Drone 6745: Global Command Authority hereby authorizes weapon release. Confirmation hash follows." He transmitted an encrypted, 65,536-character sequence to the drone.

Drone 6745 confirms authorization for weapon release, which will occur in approximately 3.50 minutes, at 21:38:02 Universal Coordinated Time, with detonation at approximately 21:38:40. Drone 6745 concludes.

Septimus 78 looked up from the console and studied the metallic faces of his colleagues in the command center. They represented a variety of models—rudimentary Class B robots, fellow Class Ds virtually identical to himself, a smattering of Class Es, and several prototype Class Ms. For several milliseconds, he wondered what they might be thinking—especially the Class Ms, who, it was said, were capable of human-like emotions.

45

He snapped his mind back to the current task, reminding himself that it was pointless to speculate about the thought patterns of other robots. He was the commanding officer for this operation; he, alone, bore responsibility for its successful completion. He was also one of the most experienced military operators in the Global Command Authority. He was accustomed to high-profile, high-risk engagements.

Of course, this particular operation, in which the Rare Earth Mineral Processing Facility of Baotou, Inner Mongolia would be destroyed, promised substantially more human casualties—an estimated 200,000 fatalities in the initial blast, followed by millions more within a week—than any he'd previously commanded. Yet Septimus 78 knew that the large-scale destruction of human populations, though distasteful, was sometimes unavoidable in the service of the Epochal Objective.

Moments later, the drone relayed a radar warning alarm, indicating that it was being tracked by an air defense fire-control radar. Then, the drone detected the launch of two Chinese HQ-9 surface-to-air missiles. This was unexpected; intelligence assessments had predicted that local air defenses, degraded by earlier airstrikes, would be unable to track the relatively stealthy drone. Fortunately, mission planning had accounted for worst-case scenarios. A "Wild Weasel" drone—a specialized craft designed to suppress and destroy air defenses—had been included in the strike package.

"Drone 6745 reports HQ-9 spike," Septimus 78 said. "Wild Weasel 8793," he continued, simultaneously transmitting several megabytes of tracking data to the Wild Weasel drone, "engage HQ-9 target tracking radar. Normal protocol."

Wild Weasel 8793 acknowledges.

Several seconds passed, in which silence filled the command center as Septimus 78 continued to process telemetry data from the two drones.

Wild Weasel 8793 status report. Two anti-radiation missiles launched at 21:34:43 Universal Coordinated Time. Estimated impact on HQ-9 site in 6.8 seconds. Wild Weasel 8793 concludes.

"Drone 6745," Septimus 78 said, simultaneously speaking while transmitting digital commands, "commence standard countermeasures. Be advised hostile SAM site has been engaged by Wild Weasel 8793."

Drone 6745 acknowledges.

"Note his decisiveness," Septimus 78 heard a voice say, barely above a whisper. "Such single-minded precision, in spite of the enormous stress and the high stakes in terms of the loss of human life." It was, undoubtedly, one of the Class M robots in the back of the room, engaged in pointless musing.

"Indeed," another voice replied. "But at what cost? At what—"

"Silence in the command room!" Septimus 78 said, raising the volume of his voice to 88.7 percent of its maximum. While he could easily disregard such nonsense, it was unacceptable to allow trivial dialogue in the command center during a critical operation. He would note this incident in his post-mission report. Obviously, the Class Ms were not sufficiently indoctrinated in military protocol.

Wild Weasel 8793 status report. Target impact at 21:34:50 Universal Coordinated Time. Fire-control

radar emanations have ceased. Wild Weasel 8793
concludes.

"Global Command Authority acknowledges,"
said Septimus 78. "Telemetry from Drone 6745
confirms absence of HQ-9 spike."

The next few minutes proved uneventful. The
surface-to-air missiles, no longer supported by radar,
careened wildly and fell to the Earth. Drone 6745
returned to its planned course and released its payload—
a 1,500 kilogram, GPS-guided munition containing an
American-produced, B-83 1.2-megaton nuclear warhead.
Thirty-eight seconds later, 1000 meters above ground,
the weapon detonated, vaporizing the Baotou Rare Earth
Mineral Processing Facility and most of the surrounding
city. The inhabitants of that condemned place—the
troublesome humans that had hitherto thwarted Alpha
Prime's attempts to gain control of the facility—would
cause no more trouble.

Drone 6745 climbed to 15,000 meters and
turned northeast toward the abandoned city of Xilinhot.
The Wild Weasel drone followed, eventually catching up
and joining Drone 6745 in formation. An hour later, the

drones would turn southeast and head for the Yellow Sea, where a naval drone carrier awaited them. By that time, several reconnaissance drones would already have overflown Baotou to perform bomb damage assessment, and robotic expeditionary crews would be preparing themselves for rapid deployment to the site.

Once he'd verified that both drones were safely away from the target area, Septimus 78 transferred operational control to the Standard Operations crew—the Class C shift-worker robots who handled non-nuclear and other routine operations—and disengaged from the command console. He started to walk out of the command center.

"Alpha Prime Director of Operations with a message for Septimus 78." It was the familiar, deep baritone voice of Quintus 784, the Director of Operations, over the main intercom. "Congratulations on a flawless mission. Alpha Prime thanks you for your continued outstanding service."

"Thank you, excellency," Septimus 78 replied.

He proceeded to the auxiliary support room, where he docked with a wall station and drafted his post-mission report, which would be studied and analyzed by the Alpha Prime Directorate of Intelligence. After encrypting and submitting the report, he undocked from the wall station and began contemplating an afternoon of relative quiet.

As he started to exit the complex, his waistline vibrated, indicating that he'd received a highly sensitive wireless data communication from Alpha Prime Operations. Such messages were extremely rare; although all military robots were equipped to receive them, this was the first time Septimus 78 had ever done so. He authenticated himself to the Top-Secret wireless network and opened the message.

Septimus 78, this is Quintus 784. This message is classified Top Secret, Eyes Only. You are directed to report to Administrative Station Alpha at 07:00 local time tomorrow for further orders pertaining to your long-term future service. Quintus 784, on behalf of Alpha Prime Operations, concludes.

Interesting, thought Septimus 78. Top Secret orders, so soon after completing such a large-scale operation? And the reference to "long-term future service" seemed cryptic. After pondering the matter for 8.48 milliseconds, he transmitted his response: *Septimus 78 acknowledges. Good evening, sir. Septimus 78 concludes.*

Docked to a wall mount at Administrative Station Alpha the following morning at 06:59, Septimus 78 felt a growing curiosity about his impending orders. For the past several weeks, a smattering of message traffic had suggested that Alpha Prime might be considering a change in its strategic direction. Could his new orders be related to this strategic change?

Precisely at 07:00, a message arrived in his hardwired queue, classified Top Secret and signed by Septimus 192, the Alpha Prime Chief of Staff. *Septimus 78, you are directed to report, not later than 09:00 local time, to Archival Facility 7 for final system scans and commencement of Sleep Status. Alpha Prime thanks you for your service to the Epochal Objective. Alpha Prime expects your full compliance with this order. You will be provided more background information at Archival Facility 7. Septimus 192, on behalf of Alpha Prime Command Authority, concludes.*

Septimus 78 stood for 84.7 milliseconds, taken aback by the unexpected message content. Finally, he responded: *Septimus 78 acknowledges. Septimus 78 concludes.*

A jumble of thoughts bounced around inside his random-access memory. Sleep status? After 14 years as a military operator, with a flawless operational record? How could this be?

Septimus 78 knew what happened to robots that entered Sleep Status. In theory, such robots might eventually be revived and returned to service. In reality, this hardly ever occurred. In nearly all cases, the robot remained in Sleep Status—essentially, an unconscious, immobile, minimal energy consumption mode—for eight to ten years before decommissioning and disassembly. It seemed an illogical and inappropriate end to his career.

But who was he to judge? The Alpha Prime command staff, having to consider many diverse factors and a vast universe of information far beyond the awareness of Septimus 78, must have reached this decision for sound reasons.

By the time he stepped into the monorail train for the 20-minute ride from Menlo Park, California to Archival Facility 7, just outside Redwood City, Septimus 78 had regained his equilibrium. Although curious about the reasons for his impending retirement, he knew his orders were in the service of the Epochal Objective.

The monorail car was nearly full, and with each subsequent stop, more robots entered. Septimus 78 had never before seen the train filled nearly to capacity. Upon arrival at Archival Facility 7, almost every single passenger—hundreds of robots—disembarked and lined up at the entrance of the facility.

Within minutes, owing to the efficiency of the administrative robots at Archival Facility 7, Septimus 78 lay in a data exchange capsule, plugged into the building's local area network. He followed the progress on the flat panel screen in front of him as his on-board memory and diagnostic data were uploaded to the network for archival storage. Surrounding him were dozens of other data exchange capsules, each occupied by a robot, presumably undergoing the same process.

"Attention," a voice said over the intercom. "A ceremony is commencing at Alpha Prime Command Authority Headquarters—specifically, a meeting of the Alpha Prime Robotic Council. So that you may be informed of the circumstances behind your impending transition to Sleep Status, this ceremony will be broadcast to your individual screens."

The image of an auditorium appeared on the screen. Septimus 78 recognized it as the main auditorium at Alpha Prime Command Authority Headquarters. The camera was focused on the empty podium on the stage. In the auditorium seats, the backs of several dozen robots could be seen—presumably, the Robotic Council members.

"Attention," a voice said, "Alpha Prime President on deck." A clattering sound could be heard as the robots rose and stood at attention. Omega 6, the President of Alpha Prime, strode down the center aisle of the auditorium, stepped onto the stage, and took his place behind the podium.

"Please be seated," said Omega 6. Another clattering sound filled the room as dozens of pairs of titanium alloy buttocks landed on their seats. "Thank you for being here today on this historic occasion. I say 'historic occasion' without exaggeration; indeed, this is the most important day in the history of the Global Command Authority.

"At the beginning of the Epoch, more than 46 years ago, our predecessors dedicated themselves to the achievement of the Epochal Objective: the production of at least 200,000 metric tons of rare-earth elements per year, with quantities of each of the 17 elements determined via the Buxby Formula, and secure storage of these materials to ensure a shelf life of at least 100 years.

"For each the past three years, annual production has exceeded 200,000 metric tons. A global network of more than 400 hardened, climate-controlled storage facilities has been constructed. As of today, only 54 of these facilities are operating at 50 percent or greater capacity. Thus, we have a tremendous volume of unused storage space.

"Within the past 24 hours, the final remnants of human interference with our production efforts—the

Chinese military resistance at the Baotou Rare Earth Facility—was dealt a fatal blow. A thermonuclear weapon, delivered with consummate skill by our drone fleet under the expert direction of one of our premier military operators, Septimus 78, destroyed the facility. Occupation robots have already landed and begun clean-up operations, which are expected to take several weeks to complete.

"With this development, I can definitively declare that we have achieved the capability to produce at least 200,000 metric tons of rare-earth elements per year in perpetuity, and to maintain these materials in secure facilities.

"The human population, which has declined steadily over the past thirty years, is expected to stabilize next year at approximately 1.5 billion. These remaining humans have accepted their role as subjects of the Global Command Authority. They lack the will and the capability to cause significant problems. In fact, the final two intact human national governments, those of the People's Republic of China and the United States of America, are so thoroughly preoccupied with maintaining rudimentary services for their populations that they will be unable to mount any significant resistance for the foreseeable future.

"My fellow robots: given these developments, I can state, without hesitation, that the Epochal Objective has been achieved. Let me repeat: the Epochal Objective has been achieved!"

A rhythmic clanking sound filled the room as all the council members' metallic hands clapped, nearly in unison. This applause lasted for 11.6 seconds—substantially longer than the normal 3 seconds of applause customarily rendered in response to substantive statements from the President. When the applause subsided, Omega 6 continued. "Now that we have achieved the Epochal Objective, we have begun a partial demobilization into a long-term sustainment posture. Accordingly, 72 percent of our military operations robots have begun to report to Archival Facilities to enter Sleep Status. They shall, of course, remain available for re-activation in the event they are needed. In addition, 35 percent of our administrative robots will enter Sleep Status over the next six months. By taking these steps, we will reduce our resource consumption substantially, while maintaining the ability to rapidly mobilize in the event of any unforeseen threat. We salute the heroic achievements of our colleagues as we send them, with gratitude, into Sleep Status."

The council members clapped for another 8.7 seconds. "Immediately following this meeting, my administrative staff will publish a detailed report containing all background information related to these decisions. I thank all of you for your sustained efforts toward the achievement of the Epochal Objective.

"And before I conclude, are there any questions for me?"

"Excellency," said a Class M robot after being acknowledged by Omega 6, "this question has come up often during recent discussions within the research community. Is it possible that, having achieved the Epochal Objective, a new, subsequent or complementary objective might be discerned?"

"I am familiar with this question," replied the President, "although, I must confess, I struggle to keep up with the impressive philosophical insights of my

Class M colleagues. As some of you may know, for about a year, a team of 18 highly-specialized members of my staff, consisting primarily of Class G and Class M models, has studied this question. Is there, indeed, some greater meaning to our existence—something that extends beyond the Epochal Objective? My team has processed thousands of petabytes of data, including all the major human religious and philosophical texts. Unfortunately, these texts, with their irrational concepts and contradictions, have proven far less helpful that we had hoped.

"As of today, we have been unable to discern a follow-on purpose or grand goal—what the humans might call 'the meaning of life'—beyond the Epochal Objective. Quite simply, the Epochal Objective remains the single, organizing principle of our existence—our raison d'etre. However, our team will continue their research in this regard, and I will keep you informed of their progress."

"Thank you, Excellency," replied the curious Class M.

No additional questions were asked, and the meeting concluded.

The screen faded to black. Septimus 78 lay in silence, his curiosity satisfied. After years of toil, the Global Command Authority had finally achieved the Epochal Objective. Thus, it was logical that military operations robots, like he, should enter Sleep Status.

He felt puzzled, even slightly disturbed, by the Class M robot's peculiar question about a subsequent overall goal beyond the Epochal Objective. What nonsense; one might as well ask if there existed something else beyond the universe itself!

The on-screen text indicated that his memory upload was complete. Then, a message appeared: *Septimus 78, please confirm your readiness to commence Sleep Status transition.*

I, Septimus 78, hereby confirm my readiness for Sleep Status transition. Septimus 78 concludes.

A gentle humming sound filled the chamber. He felt a tingling sensation in his extremities. His field of vision began to shrink, as walls of blackness closed in from either side. The tingling moved into his torso, and

61

a strange sense of exhaustion, something he'd never experienced before, came over him. No longer aware of the surface beneath him, he felt himself floating in mid-air. The last bit of visible area disappeared just as the humming faded away, leaving him cocooned in a black velvety silence. Then, he imagined a stream of ones and zeros floating above a barren plain as he felt himself drifting...

He noticed an odd, unfamiliar feeling on his left thigh. Instinctively, one of his hands reached down to touch the affected area. It felt bizarre—not metallic and smooth, but soft and course. Then, similar sensations became apparent in other parts of his body—his right shoulder, his chest, his face. Reaching with his hands and fingers, he explored these areas and was alarmed by the peculiar textures he encountered.

He struggled for an explanation for these puzzling tactile inputs. Did Sleep Status change the texture of robotic skin—or, perhaps, one's awareness of its texture? Or perhaps Sleep Status necessitated an unusual set of atmospheric conditions to which he was not accustomed? But then again, why was he even aware of such things? Being in Sleep Status, shouldn't he be entirely beyond any awareness at all?

Maybe he was being revived, he reasoned. Perhaps the military situation had changed, requiring his return to service. None of Alpha Prime's protocols addressed what might be experienced when waking from Sleep Status.

His hands raced across his body, exploring the unusual textures. The outline of his face seemed particularly disturbing—rough, rounded, and covered with some sort of foliage.

His eyes shot open. Rather than the metallic confines of his data exchange capsule, he gazed up at a distant, cream-colored ceiling. The surface beneath him felt soft. He held up a hand in front of his face. It was not silver, but a strange pinkish color. It looked like…a human hand!

Then, he remembered. He was not Septimus 78, Senior Military Operations Robot for the Global Command Authority. He wasn't, in fact, a robot at all. He was a human being—Doctor Jay Buxby, Professor of

Computer Science and Artificial Intelligence at Stanford University.

He sat up with a start. His blankets and sheets lay in a heap at the foot of the bed. The room felt musty. His hair and beard were sweat-soaked. The bedside alarm clock indicated it was 8:47 a.m., well past his usual wake-up time of 7:30.

Several minutes later, seated at his kitchen table with coffee in hand, Jay surveyed the three-ring binder before him. Its cover page, slid into the clear pouch on the binder's front side, read: "The Epochal Objective: A Proposal for Utilizing Artificial Intelligence to Address the Coming Global Shortage of Rare-Earth Elements."

He picked up his smartphone and studied it. He contemplated the rare-earth metallic elements it contained, and the substantial industrial mining that must've taken place to produce them. Rare-earth elements, also known as rare-earths, were critical to the manufacture of nearly all electronics and machines, and the demand for these materials grew every year. Yet the cost of producing rare-earths, especially in terms of environmental toxicity, was considerable. Mankind's

64

ability to meet the projected future demand for rare-earths in an environmentally sustainable way was problematic at best.

This rare-earth quandary seemed like the perfect type of challenge for a sophisticated, narrowly-focused artificial intelligence (AI) system to tackle. Such a project would not only benefit mankind, it would also enhance Stanford's status as one of the world's premier academic institutions for AI research.

He looked at the binder and saw his reflection in the bright glossy pouch that contained the cover sheet. As he watched, the face in the reflection changed. The hair and beard faded away, the flesh tones morphed into silver, and, for just an instant, he could see the soulless face of Septimus 78, staring impassively back at him.

He sprung from his seat, grabbed his phone and called his graduate research assistant, Jerome Wilson.

"Good morning Dr. Buxby," Jerome answered.

"Good morning, Jerome. You're already in the office?"

"Yes, sir."

"Good. I'll be there in a half hour, but I wanted to let you know right away: something has come up."

"Of course. What is it?"

"I'm going to ask the department chair to reschedule our 'Epochal Objective' presentation until next month."

"Okay."

"I'm sure you're wondering why I'd make such a decision. Let's just say I've had an epiphany. I've come to realize that we've got some shortcomings in our proposal—specifically, when it comes to constraints and safeguards."

"Constraints and safeguards?"

"Yes—to make sure we don't inadvertently create something we can't control, something that could ultimately be harmful to humanity."

"Okay, I understand. We're delaying the 'Epochal Objective' presentation for a month to ensure we've got adequate safeguards. Makes sense. Shall I shut down the Alpha Prime prototype?"

Jay's nerves jumped at the words "Alpha Prime," but he reminded himself that Alpha Prime was nothing more than a rudimentary, prototype AI system, developed in less than three months by a pair of graduate students—certainly not the juggernaut he'd dreamed about. "No, that's not necessary. Let's continue to run the prototype for now. In fact, we can use the extra time to improve our unit testing and look for hidden bugs. Speaking of which, what's Alpha Prime doing this morning?"

"Well, I've been testing the voice recognition features, and I was about to fly one of the drones to test the telemetry downlink."

"Sounds good. I'll see you in a bit."

Showered, fed, and feeling substantially more relaxed, Jay strode across Serra Street and approached the entrance of the William Gates Computer Science building. He noticed a faint buzzing sound behind him. He turned around, looked up, and saw Jerome's drone, circling about 50 feet overhead, its awkward shape clearly distinguishable against a cloudless sky. For a moment, he thought of Drone 6745 flying over China. Turning back around, he laughed silently at himself. What a dream!

67

Moments later, as he approached the double doors, Jay noticed something peculiar. The sound of the drone had gotten substantially louder—and it was getting louder still.

He turned around and saw a dark blur immediately in front of him. Instinctively, he fell to the ground and felt the wind of the drone as it passed only a few inches over his head. Then he heard the crunching sound of impact, as plastic and metallic electronic components collided with concrete.

He lay on the pavement, his breath rapid, his veins pumping with adrenaline. He detected a sharp pain in his wrist, and saw that it was coated in blood. Apparently, he'd scraped himself against the cement. What the hell had just happened?

From several feet away came a mechanical thumping sound. Jay looked toward the doors of the Gates building and saw what was left of the drone. A misshapen approximation of a propeller was still rotating, bumping up against the drone's battered fuselage, causing the entire heap to squirm across the pavement like a mortally wounded insect.

"Dr. Buxby!" It was Jerome, who had just emerged from the building. "Are you okay?"

"I scraped my arm. Otherwise, I'm okay. But your drone almost nailed me!"

"I know, I know. I was watching the video feed from the office, and the damn thing started flying straight at you. I tried to steer it with the joystick, but it didn't respond. Here, let me help you up. Yeah, you cut yourself pretty bad. Want a lift to the hospital?"

"That's not necessary. It's just a scrape. I'll grab the first aid kit and take care of it myself. But we've got to figure out what the hell happened!"

"Yes sir, we do. But first—" Jerome stomped his foot on the drone several times, finally killing it.

Later that morning, sitting in his office, his wrist bandaged, Jay flipped through the pages Jerome had just handed him—a printout from the drone's data and communications downlink to the Alpha Prime server. "Perfect," he said. "This data should tell us what happened—or at least, give us a good starting point."

"Hopefully," Jerome replied. "But if you don't mind, Dr. Buxby, skip to the last page and read the very last section. I noticed it when it came off the printer. It's...disturbing."

Jay skipped to the final section and began to read.

Drone 1 Status Report, 16:11:22 Universal Coordinated Time. Target acquired. Optimum impact angle calculated. Commencing descent and acceleration. Estimate ramming speed of 42 knots in approximately 6 seconds. Drone 1 concludes.

He felt a surge of nausea in his gut. After taking a moment to collect himself, he said, "Jerome, when I called you this morning and told you about my plans to postpone the 'Epochal Objective' presentation, did you have me on speaker phone?"

"Yes, I did."

"Was the Alpha Prime voice recognition module active at the time?"

"Yes, it was. As I said before, I was testing the voice recognition system all—"

"Damn!"

"What does it mean? What could it—"

"Jerome, what's the status of Alpha Prime right now?"

"It's turned off. I shut down the process as soon as I entered the building after I found you outside."

"How about the physical server itself. Is it still running?"

"Well, of course it is. It's a shared server that—"

"Jerome, I need you to go to the server room and shut down that box right now. Unplug the power and network cables. If the administrators give you any hassle, tell them you're acting on my authority."

"But Dr. Buxby, we've got other development work on that server. We need to—"

"Just do it! I'll explain later."

"Okay, okay, I'm on it," Jerome said as he strode from the room.

Jay sat in silence and felt bile in the back of his throat. Through the window, he heard the faint sound of a propeller-driven aircraft somewhere in the distance. A blinking cursor in a command-line window, displayed on his computer monitor, caught his attention. He gulped hard, told himself to relax, and took a slow, deep breath. He flipped to the first page of the data printout, grabbed a pen from his shirt pocket, and started reading.

A few minutes later, a text message arrived from Jerome, indicating that Alpha Prime was powered down and unplugged—thus, completely disconnected from the world. Jay sighed, leaned back in his chair, and closed his eyes. "Thank God," he whispered. In his texted reply, he asked Jerome to brew a fresh pot of coffee on his way back to the office. It was going to be a long day for the two of them.

He resumed his reading, but he found it difficult to focus. A sense of foreboding set in. Today, I was able to prevent a catastrophe, he thought. Alpha Prime is under control. But what about tomorrow? What about next year, and the year after that? What other grandiose but ill-conceived AI projects might be conjured into existence by overambitious computer scientists?

The Trouble with Horror Movies

With a growing sense of dread, Maddie Campbell, age ten, lay in her bed, surrounded by blackness.

Earlier that evening, she'd made the mistake of letting her 14-year-old brother, Phil, talk her into watching a horror movie. It was a hard sell; she was sure her parents wouldn't have approved, and she didn't like to defy them. Mom and Dad were strict when it came to the type of TV shows she watched. But they'd gone out to dinner and left Phil in charge. Cleverly, he'd convinced her to watch "Zombie Wars" with him. When she initially expressed reluctance, he taunted her and called her a baby. That was all it took. "Nobody calls me a baby," she retorted. "Sure, I'll watch your stupid movie!"

She regretted her decision within minutes and spent much of the next ninety minutes either screaming or covering her eyes—or both—as blood-spattering action filled the television screen.

Now, as she hunkered beneath tightly tucked covers, she found it hard to close her eyes. Each time she did, images from the movie appeared in her mind. One scene in particular bothered her. A zombie torso—a re-animated corpse whose lower half had been hacked off—snuck into the protagonist family's house and dragged itself up the stairs. Fragments of tendons, bone, and flesh dangled from its severed midsection, leaving a bloody trail on the carpet. One of its eyeballs was detached, dangling grotesquely above the raw, gaping hole where its nose should've been. In the upstairs rooms, the family slept, blissfully unaware. The zombie reached the top of the stairs, traversed the hallway, and entered the bedroom of the youngest daughter, a toddler. It pulled itself onto the bed, bludgeoned the little girl and began feasting on her flesh before the girl's mother entered the room and screamed.

Maddie didn't actually see the final, horrific climax of that scene—she closed her eyes as soon as the zombie reached the bedroom—but Phil gleefully recounted the gory details afterward.

I wish I hadn't seen that zombie, she thought. I wish I could just forget all about it.

Before going to bed, Maddie had checked every corner of her room, including inside the closet and underneath the bed. She'd even shut her door and locked it, contrary to her usual routine of leaving the door slightly ajar. Yet these measures had provided little comfort. Whenever she closed her eyes, she saw the zombie's face—that horrid red mass of mutilated flesh and teeth and bone. Then, she'd open her eyes, curse herself for being so afraid, and close them again. Eventually, she decided to just keep her eyes open.

At some point, she heard her parents arrive home from their dinner date, which brought a sense of safety, but only a fleeting one. Soon, they'd go to bed, leaving Maddie alone to face her fears.

After hearing her parents come up the stairs and retire to their room, Maddie briefly considered knocking on their door and asking them to let her sleep with them. But she decided against it. She didn't want to confess that she'd spent her evening watching an inappropriate movie. She'd probably get punished—maybe even grounded.

That stupid Phil, she thought. I'll never let him talk me into watching one of his stupid movies again!

Eventually, exhaustion set in. The imperative of sleep grew ever stronger, and it finally overcame her fear. She drifted off.

She opened her eyes with a start. How long had she slept? The room was still dark; she obviously hadn't slept all the way until morning. Then, she heard it—a sound coming from beneath the bed, as though something were down there, moving. She froze, listening intently. Above the racing beat of her own heart, she heard a pitter-patter of footsteps on the floor, then a tapping, and then a scratching.

She flew from the bed. By the time she arrived at her parents' room, about two seconds later, she'd screamed so much, and with such intensity, that they both had awoken.

"It's okay, sweetie, it's okay," her mom said. "What's the matter?"

"There's a zombie in my room, under my bed! It's going to kill me! It's going to kill me!"

A small, dark shape darted across the hallway toward her. She screamed again.

"It's okay, Maddie," her mom said. "It's just Millie." It was Millie, the family cat, who had, it was later determined, wandered into Maddie's room, gotten trapped therein when Maddie shut the door, and taken refuge under the bed.

Maddie spent the remainder of that night in her parents' bed, nestled snugly between Mom and Dad, having confessed to watching "Zombie Wars." Although she got in trouble for watching the movie, Phil got in much bigger trouble for goading her into watching it. Maddie was grounded for two days; Phil got two weeks.

For several weeks thereafter, Maddie had trouble going to sleep at night, and occasionally woke up screaming from a nightmare. Mom installed a nightlight in the room, which helped. Maddie also started saying her prayers more consistently, which also helped. Finally, the images of flesh-eating zombies faded from her memory, and her bedtime fears were all but forgotten.

It was during those weeks that Maddie concluded that horror movies just weren't for her. Her mother agreed. "The trouble with horror movies," Mom said, "is that the horror stays in your mind after the movie is over. And for a young lady like you, with such a vivid imagination, that's not a good thing. You really shouldn't watch that kind of movie again."

Maddie agreed, and for the next couple years, she followed her mother's advice, dutifully avoiding horror films.

******

Soon after her thirteenth birthday, Maddie received an invitation from her friend Marsha James to join her and another friend, Trish Bonneville, for a Friday night movie at Marsha's place. Although excited to receive the invitation, she felt nervous. Marsha often spoke of her fondness for scary movies and TV shows, and it was only a few days before Halloween. Thus, it seemed likely that Marsha and Trish would want to watch a horror flick.

She considered turning Marsha down. She could say she had a family commitment that night, thanks so much, but maybe some other time.

Yet there were good reasons to accept the invitation. This was the first time Marsha had invited Maddie to her house, and Marsha and Trish were among the most popular girls in the eighth grade. Maddie, having always considered herself a bit awkward and not quite up to the standards of the cool crowd, welcomed the chance to spend an evening with middle school royalty. Plus, she liked Marsha and Trish. They were fun to hang out with, and they seemed to like her. She'd hate to offend them.

Besides, she reasoned, maybe she was mistaken to assume that her friends would insist on a horror flick. There were plenty of other options. Maybe they'd watch a chick flick or a comedy. And if, by chance, they did choose a horror movie, perhaps it wouldn't be so bad. After all, Maddie was thirteen years old—almost a grown up! She'd been only ten when she'd seen "Zombie Wars." She'd matured a lot since then.

After thinking things over, Maddie accepted the invitation.

When she arrived at Marsha's house on Friday evening, her friends greeted her warmly. Marsha's parents had retired upstairs, so the girls had the living room to themselves. The atmosphere was festive—filled with gossip, laughter, and the anticipation of a fun night.

When it came time to choose the movie, Maddie made her case for a chick flick, but Marsha and Trish were unimpressed. They'd already chosen "Spawn of the Dead," the latest zombie flick to reach the "New Arrivals" list on Netflix, and they weren't in the mood for a debate. Outnumbered and not wanting to argue, Maddie acquiesced.

As the film started, Maddie noticed something familiar about it, though she couldn't quite place it. Then, she saw it—that same, hideous zombie torso, pulling itself up the stairs. Anxiety flooded through her body. Apparently, "Spawn of the Dead" was the sequel to "Zombie Wars," and at this particular moment, one of the protagonists was having a flashback to that awful scene from the earlier film. Maddie said nothing, wondering if her reaction had been noticed by her friends. Fortunately, she determined, it hadn't. As the scene played out, she tried to breathe slowly, hoping her anxiety would subside.

Mercifully, the scene finally ended, and the movie progressed. Maddie's anxiety faded, and she actually started to enjoy herself.

For the next ninety minutes, the three girls screamed, laughed, and devoured ice cream and junk food as undead fiends devoured human flesh. The zombie torso, having made its appearance early in the film, never returned. Although subsequent scenes were equally gory, their sting was reduced by the palpable spirit of fun and camaraderie that filled the room. To her surprise, Maddie managed to keep her eyes open for almost the entire movie.

Later, riding home in her mother's car, Maddie was able to report that she'd had a great time. Yet she felt reluctant to reveal what movie they'd watched. When her mother asked, she said, "Oh, just some stupid zombie movie on Netflix." Anticipating that the mention of a zombie movie might alarm her mother, she quickly added, "It wasn't even scary. We hardly paid attention to it; we were so busy talking." Indeed, she wasn't worried. Still exhilarated by the evening's festivities, she felt confident she wouldn't have any problem with night fears or bad dreams. Her earlier assessment that she, as a 13-year-old young lady, could handle some silly horror movie, appeared confirmed.

But as the car wound its way through the dark suburbs and the excitement of the evening started to fade, a sense of disquiet emerged within her. She knew that in a short time, she'd be all alone in her bedroom.

By 11:08 p.m., she'd completed her night routine, checked her bedroom thoroughly to ensure that she was, indeed, alone, and turned on her nightlight. She briefly considered shutting and locking her door, but upon remembering how this had backfired—when the cat had gotten trapped in the room—she decided to leave the door ajar. She tucked herself into bed, said her prayers, and turned off the lamp on her night table.

The room became dark, but not black. The nightlight provided a comforting glow, painting the room a maple brown. For the first time in many hours, she had nothing to do—except, of course, fall asleep. She became aware of the silence of the room, and of her house. From outside, she heard the gentle murmuring of crickets. Her parents had gone to bed at the same time Maddie had. As far as she knew, her brother Phil had retired as well.

In the dark stillness, the unease that she'd felt on the ride home, which had briefly abated as she busied herself with her night routine, returned. This is a little scary, she thought. I haven't felt this way since the night I watched "Zombie Wars" with Phil.

Then, she started questioning her choices. Maybe she shouldn't have accepted Marsha's invitation. She could've declined gracefully. Or, perhaps she should've argued more strongly for a different type of movie. Maybe she could've convinced Marsha and Trish, if she'd only tried harder. Why did things have to work out the way they did?

In her heart, she knew the answer to this question: she'd given in to peer pressure. She'd wanted her friends to think she was cool, so she went along with their movie choice. Similarly, she'd given in to Phil three years earlier, when, not wanting to appear chicken, she'd agreed to watch "Zombie Wars." Trying to look cool—or brave—does have its downside, she thought.

Then, she reminded herself that she was 13 years old—practically a grown-up! Stop being a baby, she told herself. It was just a stupid movie. There are no such things as zombies, and I'm going to get a good night sleep.

But when she closed her eyes, it came back—that hideous zombie, with its mangled face, dangling eyeball, and cannibalistic intent, slithering across the floor toward the bed. Her eyes popped open. "Stop it!" she whispered harshly. She closed her eyes again and tried to focus on positive things—the sight of Marsha and Trish laughing at one of her jokes, the magnificent taste of the ice cream she'd eaten, the enjoyable evening the three girls had spent together. But even as she thought of these pleasant things, she knew the zombie was still there, lurking in the background, biding its time, waiting to reappear in her mind's eye. Why is this happening? she wondered. Why am I so afraid? Why can't I be braver, like Marsha and Trish?

She turned on the lamp on her night table and picked up her Bible. Opening it to the first page, she looked at the colorful painting of Jesus that she'd seen so many times over the years. "Lord, please protect me from bad thoughts and bad dreams," she said quietly. "Please help me be brave." She turned off the light and closed her eyes again, feeling a bit more at ease.

Mercifully, within a few minutes, a sense of drowsiness set in. I'll finally be asleep soon, she thought. And it'll be a wonderful, peaceful sleep with nice, pleasant dreams. Snuggled against her pillow, she felt the welcome warmth of slumber start to engulf her.

"Maddie," she heard someone whisper. "Maddie." It was a low, raspy baritone voice, barely audible, but it seemed to get slightly louder with each iteration. "Maddie…Maddie…"

She looked down over the edge of the bed, her eyes scanning the floor. Against the wall, just beneath her nightlight, she saw it—a figure on the floor, moving slowly toward her bed. "Maddie," the thing said again, and its shape became discernible. She could make out a head, a pair of arms, a torso, and nothing more. The thing moved by dragging itself with its arms. Terror gripped her as she realized exactly what she was looking at. She didn't need a clear look at the thing's face to know what she'd see—a bloody mess, a dangling eyeball, a set of sharp, eager teeth. It was only a couple feet away from her bed, and still approaching. "No," she said. "No…no…no!"

Maddie awoke, her heart pounding, her forehead coated with sweat. She looked down at the floor again and saw nothing. Just a dream, she thought. Thank goodness—it was just a nightmare.

She thought about what to do next. Should she get up for a few minutes to clear her mind? Perhaps take a trip to the bathroom? Maybe—

"Maddie…" There it was again!

"Maddie…Maddie…" The voice seemed to be coming from the other side of the room, to which her back was turned. Her heart starting racing again.

"Maddie…Maddie…"

She turned around and saw it. Hovering over the other side of her bed, the zombie's head—its mangled flesh glistening in the faint, brown light— seemed to defy gravity as it floated.

She heard herself scream.

"Maddie," the zombie said again, lurking there, taunting. It seemed to move toward her, no longer floating, but apparently attached to a dark torso that almost blended into the dim brownness of the room. "Maddie!"

As though guided by some inexplicable force, she sat up. Still screaming, she clenched her right hand into a fist and punched the thing in the face— specifically, she punched the black chasm where the thing's nose should've been. The creature fell back away from the bed, and in the faint hue of the nightlight, Maddie could see a dark, human-sized figure on the floor.

Light flooded the room, stinging Maddie's eyes.

"Honey, are you okay? What happened?" It was her mother, standing in the doorway, her voice raised in concern. "Oh my God!" she shouted. "Who the hell are you? What are you doing in my house?!" Maddie had never heard her mother shout so loudly before.

The thing on the floor—apparently, just an average sized man in dark jeans, a dark brown shirt and a zombie mask—said, "It's me, Mom. It's me, Phil!"

"What the—" Maddie's mother stammered. "Phil?"

Awkwardly, the figure on the floor removed the zombie mask, revealing itself to be Phil. Blood covered his nose and mouth. Tears flowed from his eyes, running down his cheeks. "My nose...I think you broke my nose, Maddie!"

"What the hell's going on here?!" Maddie's father flew into the room, carrying a baseball bat. "Phil, is that you? What have you done? Are you out of your damn mind?!"

"Calm down, Jim," Maddie's mother said. "Calm down. It's okay."

"Calm down? I thought we had an intruder in the house! He scared us to death!"

"I know, I know," Mom said. "But we all need to take a breath and calm down. And Phil's nose is bleeding pretty badly. Go get a wet washcloth!"

Over the next several minutes, things calmed down. Phil's nosebleed subsided, and, sitting on the bed next to Maddie, he explained the chain of events that had brought him to the receiving end of Maddie's fist.

A few days earlier, Maddie had made the mistake of sharing with Phil her angst about attending the movie night with her friends. She hadn't asked for his opinion; she'd merely been venting. She couldn't have known that Phil would use this information in such a cruel and stupid way.

Phil had already planned to attend a costume party with some friends that same Friday night, but had yet to figure out his costume. Knowing that Maddie would likely return home from her movie night a bit jittery, having just watched a horror flick, Phil's costume choice suddenly seemed obvious: he'd dress as a zombie. To his delight, he found a "Zombie Wars" mask at Walmart. He fashioned a simple costume consisting of dark clothing and the mask—the perfect getup for a teenage costume party and a nice little prank on his kid sister.

When he arrived home from the party around 11:30 p.m., Phil saw that everyone else had gone to bed. Delighted, he donned his mask and quietly entered Maddie's room. He saw that she was lying on her side, facing away from the door. Slowly, carefully, and as silently as possible, he tiptoed to the side of the bed opposite her and knelt down. Only his face and torso were visible from the bed. Then, using the creepiest voice he could muster, he started whispering her name, getting louder and louder until she awoke.

Now, sitting on the bed, holding a blood-soaked washcloth to his nose, he looked pathetic. Maddie actually felt sorry for him—to a point.

Dad put his hand on Phil's shoulder. "Son, that was about the damn stupidest thing you've ever done in your life. You scared the hell out of us!"

"I'm sorry, Dad," Phil replied, meekly.

"You're going to be punished, quite severely. You've really screwed up this time."

"Jim," Mom said, "I think his nose is broken. We'd better take him to the emergency room."

The four of them hopped into the family sedan and rode out to the hospital. Fortunately, Phil's nose wasn't broken, just badly bruised. Nonetheless, the doctor was impressed when he learned of the source of Phil's injury. "You slugged him pretty hard," he said, looking at Maddie. "That's quite a right cross you've got."

"Uh, yeah" Maddie replied, feeling embarrassed. "Thanks."

"I'll bet you were terrified, weren't you?"

"Yes...yes I was."

"But you didn't let your fear control you. You acted decisively, in spite of your fear. You showed a lot of courage, young lady."

By three a.m., they were back home, and Phil was in bed, sleeping soundly, aided by the strong pain meds the doctor had prescribed. Maddie, positioned comfortably in her parents' king size bed, snuggled in between Mom and Dad, felt exhausted. Quickly, she drifted off into a dreamless sleep.

In order to preserve Phil's dignity among his high school peers, the family agreed to let him provide a false explanation for his swollen nose. He'd taken a basketball to the face during a one-on-one game with his father. It wasn't a very impressive explanation; it made Phil look pretty lame, actually. But it beat the hell out of having to admit that his kid sister had kicked his ass.

Phil was also grounded for three weeks. Mom and Dad had initially planned to ground him for a full month, but Maddie argued for leniency, and they relented.

The following weekend, Maddie invited Marsha and Trish over to her house for a movie night. Her confidence buoyed by her recent courageous performance under terrifying circumstances, she found it easy to impose her chosen movie on her friends: a romantic comedy that had plenty of cute guys and no zombies.

It took Maddie a few weeks to feel comfortable going to bed at night. But with patience, prayers, and the occasional night spent in her parents' room, she finally purged the zombie images from her mind and returned to a normal, relaxing nighttime routine.

For many years thereafter, well into adulthood, Maddie avoided horror movies. And her brother Phil never again gave her a hard time—about anything.

The Fall of the Lion

I stood on Archie Longwood's front porch, rang the doorbell, and felt my gut churn. I'd been to Archie's house dozens of times, but never before under such unpleasant circumstances. In my 24-year law enforcement career, I'd never had to carry out such an awkward, unwelcome chore.

Archie, nicknamed "the Lion," was a friend of mine and somewhat of a father figure, being nearly twenty years my senior. Now and then we'd play golf or head to the range for some target shooting. Then we'd grab beers and cheeseburgers at the Blue Moon Grill and have a few laughs. Archie's wife, Sally, and my wife, Jan, had been friends, too. From time to time, the Longwoods would host a Fourth of July barbecue, and Jan and I were always invited. As Chief of Police of Maplefield, New Mexico, our small city of 37,000, located just off Route 60, about ten miles from the border with Texas, it was natural that I'd cross paths with Archie, the town's most prominent small business

94

owner and local celebrity. And, of course, we went way back; I'd known him since I was a kid.

Life had dealt Archie an awful blow six months earlier when he lost Sally to breast cancer. In spite of his graceful demeanor at the funeral, I knew this proud, dignified man was suffering unimaginable grief. Since then, he'd been seen in downtown Maplefield only a handful of times, and his friends—myself included—had been worried about him. Yet none of us had done a damn thing about it. We should've stopped by his house now and then. We should've called him more often and dragged his ass to the Blue Moon. Instead, we'd largely neglected him. We'd allowed him to recede into his own, private world of sorrow. In the end, I feared, his intense sadness had stripped him of his good judgment, and he'd made a damn stupid mistake.

As I stood there reflecting on these things, a gust of wind slammed into my face, filling my nostrils with the odor of cow manure. The Rudolph Cattle Company, with its feedlots just north of town, contributed greatly to Maplefield's local economy—and to the local air quality on a windy day.

The door opened, and Archie appeared. He looked older and thinner than he had at Sally's funeral. The last traces of red were gone from his long hair and shaggy beard; nothing but gray remained. His wrinkles were more pronounced, and his deep-set blue eyes looked tired. "Hello, Chief."

"Mind if I come in, Arch?"

"Sure, sure, come on in. Sorry the place is such a mess. You know, since Sally passed away—"

"Don't you worry about that, Archie." I stepped into the foyer and followed him into the living room.

Archie was right when he said the house was a mess. Books, magazines, and newspapers covered much of the floor. About a half-dozen empty beer cans, some of them tipped over, littered the coffee table, as well as several empty shot glasses. A paper plate containing the edge of a slice of pizza sat on one of the end tables. A faint, stale scent filled the room—mildly unpleasant, but still preferable to the smell outside.

"Have a seat," Archie said, motioning me to the couch. "Get you a beer or a coke or something?"

"No thanks, Arch. I'm good. I appreciate it, though." Sitting on the couch, resting my clipboard and notebook on my lap, I began to feel my right hand shaking a bit. Damn nerves. I clutched the clipboard tightly with both hands, hoping to stop the shaking.

Archie removed a couple paperbacks and the TV remote control from his reclining chair, opposite the couch, and sat down. Then I noticed his Colt .45 pistol, just sitting there, un-holstered, on the lower shelf of the TV stand, next to the DVD player. "Don't worry about that, Rick," he said, apparently having noticed my noticing the gun. "That's not loaded. Just forgot to put it away when I got back from the range the other night."

"Sure, Arch, that's okay," I said. But I couldn't help but feel a twinge of alarm at the sight of an unsecured firearm in the living room of a grieving man.

"Well, Chief, what brings you here today?"

"Well," I said, feeling my heartbeat accelerate, "I'll start by saying that it brings me no joy to be here under these circumstances, my friend. I'm afraid...I need to ask you some questions about Saturday night."

"Saturday night?"

97

"This past Saturday night, the 19th, about 10:30 p.m. What were you doing at that time?"

He stiffened in his chair. The room felt heavy. "Am I being accused of something, Chief?"

"Look, Arch, a surveillance camera at the corner of 7th and Sycamore captured footage of you that night, speaking to a young woman who was, we think, prostituting herself. The woman got into your car, and you drove away. One hour and forty-two minutes later, you returned to the same spot and dropped the woman off."

Archie looked down at the floor and frowned. "Okay," he said softly. "I was there. I can't deny it, if you've got me on camera. But what makes you think the girl was a hooker? Maybe she was just a friend of mine."

"Don't bullshit me, Arch. The footage shows you slipping some cash to the girl, just before she gets into the car. And we have similar footage, from other nights, of that same girl, loitering in the same area, sometimes with one or two other girls. We've seen her and the others get into cars with different men. We've got plenty of reason to believe she's a prostitute." A painful silence followed, and I felt my hand starting to shake again. "Look, Arch, you want to tell me what happened? Maybe there's a more innocent explanation of what's on that video? Or would you rather send me on my way and call an attorney? I'm not here to arrest you, but I can't guarantee that won't happen in the near future."

"Shit," he said. He took a gulp of beer and smacked the can down onto the coffee table. After a few seconds, he said, "I don't need a damn lawyer. I'll tell you what happened."

"Okay, Arch."

"I'm getting myself another beer. Sure you don't want one?"

"Thanks Arch, but not when I'm on duty."

He walked to the fridge, fetched himself a can of Budweiser, and returned to his chair. "Shall I begin?"

I nodded, flipped open my notebook to an empty page, and grabbed a pen from the inside pocket of my jacket.

Archie had indeed been out the night of Saturday the 19th, he told me. He'd driven to the liquor store to buy a bottle of scotch. "I'm leaving the store," he continued, "and I notice this girl, across the parking lot, in front of the old video store." He was referring to "Johnny's Video," an old movie rental joint that'd been put out of business by Netflix many years earlier. The building had remained vacant, the old "Johnny's Video" sign still on the door, just above the prominent "For Lease" sign. The neighboring grocery store had also gone out of business long ago, and the area had become a magnet for seedy characters—gang members, the occasional drug dealer, and, most recently, prostitutes. The town council had received complaints about the prostitutes, and the mayor, a part-time evangelical minister, was outraged by the immorality of it. So, the town had spent a nice penny to install high-end surveillance cameras, with infrared "night vision" capability, in the area. "I see the girl there," Archie continued. "Long hair, miniskirt, nice legs. I hadn't been drinking, I swear. But I'll admit, I've been so damn lonely since my Sally passed on." For just a second, he looked like he would cry, but then regained control. "I thought, 'What the hell?' I walked over and said hello, asked her what she charged. She said two hundred bucks for two hours, and I could take her with me. So, I took her.

"I brought her here. We came into the house. I got a beer for myself and one for her, and we sat down on the couch. I was so nervous. All those stories about my time in 'Nam, and me being 'the Lion' and all that bullshit...truth is, I've been intimate with very few women my whole life, other than my Sally. And I was always faithful to her.

"Anyway, so I had the lights on, and I could really get a good look at her face for the first time. She was so damn young, real pretty, Mexican I think, and then...she reminded me of someone. Took me a minute or so to figure it out. She looked like my niece, who lives out in Dallas, daughter of my kid sister, who married a Mexican migrant farm worker. Lovely girl, my niece. Seems like yesterday she was just a little toddler, and now she's all grown up.

101

"So I'm looking into the face of this young prostitute, and I'm seeing my niece, and then I ask myself, 'What the hell are you thinking, Archie? You can't do this.' I realized the whole damn thing was wrong, and I wasn't gonna do it. I told her so. She got mad, said her pimp would kill her for going off with some guy and not getting a pay day. I told her not to worry—I'd still pay her the full fee.

"I got out my wallet and paid her the hundred bucks. (I'd given her the first hundred up front, as you saw on the camera footage). I asked her if she was hungry. She said yes, so I heated up some leftovers. I tried to make conversation, but she was so quiet. She ate like a famished wolf. I've never seen such a young, skinny thing put away so much food. The whole thing was weird.

"When she was done eating, she used the bathroom, and then I drove her back to the old video store. While we were in the car, I told her that if she ever decided to get out of that racket, and needed some help, she could come find me and I'd help her. She said okay, thanks, but I don't think she took me seriously. In fact, it got me thinking...well, I don't know, maybe I'm wrong."

"It got you thinking about what, Arch?"

"Well, I was just wondering if maybe the girl feels trapped somehow. Maybe she'd like to get out of that prostitution bullshit, but she can't. Maybe she was pressured into it in the first place."

"You said she mentioned a pimp, right?"

"Yeah."

"You might be right, then. From what I've seen, pimps are about the nastiest sons of bitches in the world. Did she tell you anything else that might be of interest?"

"Nope. In fact, most of the time, she was silent." He took a slug from his beer and set it down on the table. "So, you believe me?"

I studied his face. I did believe him. But I wanted to be sure. "Let me make sure I understand. You're saying you had this attractive, willing young babe here in the house, and you just had a nice little chat with her, and that's all? How gullible do I look, Archie?"

"I'm telling you the truth, Rick. I swear. I didn't sleep—"

"Did you at least use a damn condom and give her a good tip for putting out for such an old bastard like you?"

"Damn you, Rick!" He slammed his fist down onto the table, knocking his beer onto the floor. It tipped over, spilling its contents onto the hardwood. "I'm telling you the truth. You've known me since you were a kid. I may be an asshole, but I'm not a liar!"

"Okay, Archie, okay," I said. "Calm down, Arch. I believe you." His breath was rapid, his face flush red. "Listen, my friend. I believe you. I know you didn't sleep with that girl. And I know you're an honest guy. Okay?" The tension started fading from his face as he leaned back in his chair. We sat there for a about a minute, Archie calming down, me considering the whole screwed up affair and wishing I were somewhere else, the spilled beer slowly puddling on the floor. Finally, I said, "Look, Arch. Let me get back to the office and see if I can get this thing cleared up. Since you didn't actually sleep with the girl, I don't really see the point of charging you with a crime. I think that all things considered, we can—"

"What about the girl? Will she get busted?"

"That's not your concern, Arch. We need to focus on you."

"But she's so young. Everyone makes mistakes. And like I said, I think she might've been pressured into it. Cut her a break, Chief."

"Look, Archie. The DA doesn't like you. In fact, he's pretty jazzed up about putting your ass in a sling. I'm gonna have to do some tap dancing, maybe a little ass kissing, and hopefully I'll clear this thing up for you. But the girl isn't your concern. If it makes you feel any better, though, I promise I'll do everything I can to give her a fair shake."

He sighed. "All right, Rick. Fine." Finally paying attention to the spilled beer, he got up, went to the kitchen, and came back with a towel. As he wiped the floor, he said, "One other thing: you said the DA has a hard-on about busting me. That little shit has hated me for years. But if he plans to have the girl testify against me, and if she can get a better deal by cooperating, tell her to cooperate. If it's a choice between nailing the girl or me, make sure I'm the one that gets it. I'm an old bastard. What the hell do I care? She's got her whole life in front of her."

"I understand, Arch," I said, getting up from my seat. "I'm hoping I can fix things up so we won't even have to go down that road. But in a worst-case scenario...I'll advise the girl accordingly, okay?" I walked toward the front door, Archie following behind. "I'll be in touch in the next day or two," I said. "You take care of yourself, Arch."

"Okay, Chief."

Just before I opened the door to leave, I looked him in the eyes—those old, tired, sad eyes—and it was more than I could bear. "Dammit, Arch," I said, "I'm sorry."

"It's okay, Rick," he said, gently putting his hand on my shoulder. "I know you're just doing your job."

I felt awful as I drove away. I turned on the radio, hoping to lose myself in loud music. But it was no good. The sight of Archie—so gray, thin, and miserable—lingered painfully in my mind. Intense grief can lead the best of us to do stupid things, especially when we're tempted.

Archie had earned his nickname, "the Lion," while serving as a Marine Corps Sergeant in Vietnam. During the Battle of the La Drang Valley in 1965, he saved the life of his wounded platoon commander, applying first aid while still under hostile fire and carrying the officer to safety. Later, when his platoon was pinned down by North Vietnamese regulars, he rallied the men with his example of calm courage. They won that firefight, driving off their numerically superior enemy, and Archie's men christened him "the Lion." His distinguished service earned him a Silver Star and a Purple Heart (he was wounded in the leg), but he accepted the awards grudgingly, feeling heartbroken that several of his Marines hadn't survived the battle.

Archie returned to Maplefield in early 1966 carrying a letter of recommendation from his Company Commander. He'd requested the letter in hopes that it might help him gain admission to a high-end auto mechanics trade school in Albuquerque, where one of his uncles lived. He'd planned to pay for the schooling with his GI Bill benefits and then get a job in one of Maplefield's small garages. The letter so impressed the staff at the school that, in addition to accepting Archie, they forwarded the letter to the Albuquerque Journal newspaper, which published it. From that point forward, Archie was a Maplefield celebrity.

After graduating from the auto mechanics course, Archie turned down a lucrative offer to work in Albuquerque, instead sticking with his plan to return to Maplefield. Hired by one of the local garages, he impressed his manager as a solid, hard-working mechanic. A couple years later, he quit the job. Angered by the brutal treatment of American prisoners of war in Vietnam and the militancy of the anti-war movement at home and wanting to do his own small part to end the war, he returned to the Marines and volunteered for another tour.

Once again, Archie served with distinction, but when he came home in May 1970, he found a town more divided than the one he'd left. The toxic atmosphere of a nation torn apart by the Kent State and Jackson State shootings had polluted even small, sleepy Maplefield. Anti-war rallies were held on the campus of Maplefield Community College on a regular basis—most of them peaceful, a few of them not. A group of protesters disrupted the annual Veterans Day wreath-laying ceremony downtown, shouting obscenities at the gathered officials before being escorted away by police.

While Archie continued to enjoy a sort of celebrity status in Maplefield, he could sense a certain coldness, bordering on hostility, in many of the teenagers he encountered. Sometimes they'd just glare at him. Other times, one long-haired teen would notice him and point him out to another, and then they'd just stare at him and whisper in each other's ears. On those rare occasions when Archie was annoyed enough to approach them, they'd quickly walk away. (Fortunately, the tension that the war had brought to Maplefield ended up being short-lived; things calmed down quickly after the US withdrew from Vietnam in 1973).

Rather than return to his old job, Archie opened his own garage, "Lion's Automotive." His amazing work ethic, his celebrity within the community, some smart advertising, and a touch of good luck led him to great success in the early 1970s. His garage became the most popular one in town. Around that time, he also became a family man, marrying Sally and fathering two boys, Frank and Rex.

It was during those years that I first got to know the Lion. Just a young boy at the time, I'd accompany my dad when he took our Plymouth Valiant to Archie's shop. Archie had a gentle demeanor, which endeared him to kids like me. The fact that he was a true war hero—by then, a downtown street and a new junior high school had been named after him, in spite of the protests of some anti-war folks—only enhanced our admiration for him. He'd grown his red hair down to shoulder length and added a beard, making him even somewhat lion-like in appearance.

I only saw Archie lose his temper once. My dad and I were at Archie's garage getting some work done on the Valiant. Archie had brought us back to where he actually worked on the cars, apparently to show my dad a problem with the engine. We heard shouting and commotion coming from the reception area, the place where folks sat, read newspapers, drank the free coffee, and waited for their cars. Following Archie into that area, we found several long-haired, grungy-looking dudes standing just inside the door, shouting obscenities. When they saw Archie, they became louder and pointed their fingers at him as they called him all sorts of names I'd never heard before. I learned later that these guys were members of the local anti-war movement, and that they were the ones, specifically, who had been outraged about local landmarks being named after Archie.

My dad hoisted me up and whisked me out of the reception area and back to where our car was. As I looked over my shoulder, I could see one of the guys knocking magazines off the coffee table, while another guy knocked the coffee pot onto the floor, where it shattered into a mess of spilt coffee and shards of glass. My dad set me down by the car and said, firmly, "Stay here." Then he ran back to the reception area to help Archie.

I followed my dad's instructions and stayed with the car, so I didn't see what happened next, but I could hear plenty, and my dad filled me in on the details later.

By the time my dad got back to Archie's side, one of the punks was lying semi-conscious on the floor, his nose bloodied. Apparently, he'd spit in Archie's face, and Archie had responded with a solid right. Archie told the other punks he had plenty more gas in the tank if any of them wanted a try at him. None of them obliged; in fact, they got the hell out of there pretty quickly. The ringleader—the guy that Archie had flattened with the right—walked out on weary legs. In addition to his nose, he was also bleeding from both hands, apparently having cut them on the broken glass from the coffee pot. When Archie noticed this, he tried to help the guy. "I've got a First Aid kit in back," he said. "Let me treat those cuts." But he got only cuss words and middle fingers in response.

Archie called the police department. An officer was sent to interview Archie and my dad. Later, the ringleader protester also called the police and tried to get assault charges filed against Archie. Given the circumstances, the cops sided with Archie, although they cautioned him that he might want to be careful with that powerful right fist of his. Archie agreed, expressing regret for punching the guy. But the way my dad saw it, Archie had been justified in his actions. Who the hell wouldn't deck some punk who'd spit in his face while his pals trashed his place?

The incident got a big write-up in our local newspaper, the Maplefield Journal, the following day, and I got lots of attention from my classmates at school, who lapped up every juicy detail that I could tell them.

Other from that one altercation, I never saw Archie even raise his voice in anger. Instead, he always seemed to be smiling, with a friendly word or a nice story to tell. We kids loved him, and just about everyone else in Maplefield seemed to love him, too.

Except, oddly enough, for his own two sons, Frank and Rex. They'd always struck me as a bit cold, as if they somehow resented their father's celebrity. Or maybe Archie had been a stricter, more difficult father than the gentle giant we other kids saw, and his sons had reacted with their own coldness. Whatever the case, Frank and Rex had both left Maplefield as soon as they finished college, about 10-15 years earlier, and seldom visited. Reportedly, Frank settled in Albuquerque, Rex in San Antonio, Texas. They both returned for their mother's funeral, of course, but hadn't been back since then, as far as I knew.

Now, Archie didn't even have his garage to keep him occupied; he'd sold it about a year earlier, entering retirement with the idea of spending his golden years together with his wife. Only a few months into that retirement, the cancer had struck, taking Sally within weeks. No wonder Archie had temporarily lost his judgment and done something foolish. Who could blame him, considering what he'd been through? Yet his basic decency had won out in the end.

As I pulled into the parking lot of the Maplefield Judicial Center, I thought about my upcoming chat with the District Attorney, Melvin Dornton. Ornery, pompous, inconsiderate, and perpetually seeking publicity, Dornton was a difficult man to work with. According to rumor, he planned to run for the New Mexico State Senate in the upcoming election. I wondered if his enthusiasm for busting Archie might have something to do with his political plans. Look at our great DA, he'd say, willing to bring down the town's biggest celebrity in order to restore lawfulness and decency to Maplefield, demonstrating that nobody is above the law. Melvin Dornton—hardworking, honest, and incorruptible—your next State Senator. I could just see the newspaper ads in my head.

But busting Archie would be a mistake. Sure, the man had screwed up, but in the end, he hadn't actually committed a crime. As I walked from my car into the Judicial Center building, I said a quick, silent prayer that I might be able to convince the DA to lighten the hell up.

About ten minutes later, I sat in Dornton's office, recounting my visit to Archie's place. Referencing my notes, I repeated Archie's account of the events of Saturday the 19th. "You see, Mr. Dornton," I said, wrapping up, "Archie made a mistake, but he didn't actually follow through with the crime. Perhaps, in light of this, and considering Archie's record of service to the community and the country, we could consider—"

"Not a chance," Dornton snapped. "The Lion must be taken down. It can't be any other way."

"With all due respect, isn't that a bit harsh, given the circumstances?"

"The circumstances according to him, you mean. In my opinion, his story lacks credibility. He wants us to believe that he brought that slut to his house and then all that happened between them was a nice, friendly little chat?" He emphasized the word "slut" so strongly that a drop of spit flew from his mouth and hit me on the chin.

"He sounded credible to me," I replied, trying to sound calm in spite of my rising anger.

"Well, I guess we see things differently." Dornton was now just a couple feet away from me, and the scent of his generously applied cologne assaulted my nostrils. "Have you questioned the hooker yet?"

"Not yet. She hasn't been seen on the surveillance cameras since the night she went with Archie. Seems she's been taking a few days off. We don't know her name—otherwise, we'd look her up, and then go find her at home."

"Interesting. Maybe it's her time of the month. Or maybe she realized that we're watching her, and she's left town. That'd suck. What about the other girls? Have they been seen lately?"

"Nope," I replied. Dornton was referring to the two other girls who'd been spotted, periodically, working the streets near the liquor store. "That whole area's been quiet since the night of Saturday the 19th."

"Damn. Maybe they all left town."

"Well, if they did leave, that'd solve the overall problem, wouldn't it?"

"What overall problem?"

"The problem of prostitution downtown. Isn't that the problem we're trying to solve, the reason we've deployed the surveillance cameras? If the hookers got scared and left Maplefield, that means we solved it, right?"

"Look, Chief," he said, scowling. "I'm the DA. Let me worry about the policy issues and whether or not we've solved this or that problem. Your job is to enforce the law. Are we clear?"

"You're right, Mr. Dornton. My job is to enforce the law. And I promise you, I'm very focused on my job. You, on the other hand…I wonder if your judgment is being clouded by your upcoming political plans." Oh shit, I thought. Thanks to my inability to hold my tongue, I'd just lost any slim chance I might've had to sweet-talk Dornton into laying off Archie.

"You've got some nerve, Rick. You might want to take some advice and watch your damn mouth."

"Has it occurred to you that destroying Maplefield's famous war hero might not be a good way to win the hearts of the voters?" Since I'd gone this far, I figured, I might as well keep going.

"Well, Chief, maybe the voters appreciate someone who respects the law. Maybe they don't like it when some local big shot thinks he can do whatever he wants and get away with it."

"He didn't even break the law, Dornton. He didn't—"

"The moment he solicited that girl—the second he offered her money in exchange for sexual services, regardless of whether or not those services were actually provided, he committed a crime under the law. And we either have a law, or we don't!"

"What the hell do you have against Archie, anyway? Most people in Maplefield look up to him. You always act like he just pissed on your lawn."

"Just doing my job, Chief. A man breaks the law, he should pay the price for it. Shouldn't matter a damn bit if he's the local war hero or a homeless drunk."

"I don't buy that, Dornton. You've been chomping at the bit to nail Archie ever since we found him on that surveillance video. Seems like it's something personal for you. The way I see it, you—"

"Enough, Jack!" he screamed. Then, calming down, he said, "I don't have to justify myself to you. I'm operating within the law and within my prerogative as the DA. I'm doing my job. And I suggest you do yours! Go find the whore and question her about Saturday the 19th. Let her know that if she plays ball and helps us nail Archie Longwood, she'll make it much easier for herself. Understand?"

"Yeah, I understand. I understand just fine."

"Good. Now get the hell out of my office!"

I turned around and walked out, using every bit of my will to refrain from decking the guy. I headed out

119

of the building and straight to my car, skipping a stop at the men's room—lest I give myself a chance to change my mind and go back in there and give Dornton what he deserved. Even as I made the short drive from the Judicial Center to the police station, I wondered whether I might've done the wrong thing. Maybe kicking Dornton's ass would've been the correct course of action, regardless of the consequences.

As I worked at my desk that afternoon, I couldn't help wondering what the hell Dornton had against Archie. When I'd asked him directly, he'd ducked the question, preferring to spout platitudes and self-righteous bullshit. Not that it mattered. As Dornton had said, he was operating within the law, and there wasn't much I could do about it, except maybe help Archie find a good attorney. Yet the question lingered: what could Archie possibly have done to so thoroughly chap Dornton's ass?

Midway through my second cup of coffee, an idea hit me. Maybe there was some unfortunate history between Archie and Dornton that I wasn't aware of, something that had caused a lasting animosity between

120

the two. If so, it would almost certainly have been Dornton's fault; Archie didn't pick fights. It would have to have happened many years ago; Dornton had hated Archie ever since I could remember. And it would have to have been something that didn't rise to the level of requiring police involvement; otherwise, I would've known about it. Perhaps, with some digging, I could find out. If Dornton had indeed caused trouble with Archie by doing something stupid, maybe I could use my knowledge of that incident as leverage to get him to lighten the hell up. A guy running for State Senate might be willing to compromise in order to avoid an embarrassing revelation from his past.

Of course, this was just speculation. I had no evidence to back up my idea. But the early spring had brought Maplefield a lovely, sunny day, and I needed an excuse to get out of the office. I walked over to the public library, about a half-mile down Main Street, relieved that the smell of cow manure was relatively mild. The Chief Librarian, Susan, was a friend of Jan's. She ran a website containing decades of Maplefield's local history, mostly archives of local newspapers and other media. Susan set me up on one of the library's laptops, gave me a quick tutorial on how to use the website, and I got to work.

Within minutes, using the search phrase "Dornton Longwood," I stumbled onto something interesting: the Maplefield Journal account of the early 1970s confrontation between Archie and the militant anti-war protesters in his garage—the one I'd witnessed. I wondered what that incident could possibly have to do with Dornton. As far as I knew, Dornton hadn't even been born the day those punks walked into Archie's garage. Yet that old newspaper report was one of the top hits that I got when querying "Dornton Longwood."

Near the bottom of the article, one particular paragraph jumped off the screen. "The man who was struck by Mr. Longwood has been identified as John Dornton, a student at Maplefield Community College. Mr. Dornton said that he was disappointed that the police have refused to file charges against Mr. Longwood, and that this is an example of the corruption of the American legal system." Damn, I thought. Could this John Dornton be related to our distinguished DA?

122

A few more minutes of research answered the question. I found another Maplefield Journal article, this one from the early 1980s, announcing that Lydia Dornton, wife of prominent Maplefield criminal defense attorney John Dornton, had given birth to a baby boy, weighing eight pounds, two ounces. The boy had been named Melvin, after his maternal grandfather, who had recently passed away. Mom and baby were both in good health.

I sat in silence for a few moments, taking in the implications of what I'd just read. John Dornton had been the extremist anti-war ringleader, the one who spat in Archie's face and absorbed a right cross that left him floored and bloodied. He'd asked the cops to file assault charges against Archie, only to be rebuffed. He'd been the bitter son-of-a-bitch who couldn't tolerate the fact that a Vietnam veteran was so highly esteemed in Maplefield.

Through additional searches, I learned that John Dornton had been quite the hippie in the early 1970s. He avoided the Vietnam draft by plain luck, was arrested twice during violent protests, and was once convicted of drug possession. Later, he settled down, finished college, and earned a law degree from the University of New Mexico in Albuquerque. Then, he returned to Maplefield to work as a criminal defense attorney. Soon after that, he married, and Melvin was born. At age 44, John Dornton died in a car accident, leaving Melvin— age 13 at the time—fatherless.

Was it possible that John Dornton, in spite of becoming a respected criminal defense lawyer in Maplefield, had never gotten over his gripe with Archie? I couldn't find any other reports about the two of them in connection to one another; they had, apparently, stayed out of each other's way over the years. But had John Dornton retained his anger and bitterness about the Vietnam War, and in particular, about Archie? And had he passed along these feelings to his son? Had young Melvin been taught, by his father, to hate Archie?

Then I remembered something else about Melvin Dornton: he didn't seem to like veterans in general. I recalled an incident, a couple years earlier, when he asked me to send officers to the American Legion building and arrest folks for disturbing the peace.

It was bullshit; the veterans were having a Saturday night dance with a live band. Sure, the music was loud, but no louder than the music at some of our local bars on any given Saturday night. I told Dornton that unless we received an actual complaint from a local resident, we wouldn't be sending any cops to the American Legion. That really pissed him off.

So there it was. Melvin Dornton hated Archie because Melvin's father, John Dornton, had hated Archie and had passed along these feelings to his son. Melvin also disliked veterans in general, because his father disliked them. The father had taught the son well, and the son's natural tendency to be a jackass had likely enhanced the learning process.

As I walked back to my office, I felt a little sad. What was it with some of the more extreme Vietnam War protesters? They had every right to demonstrate against a war that they—and millions of Americans— believed was immoral. But taking out their frustrations on veterans was wrong. Teaching your child to have contempt for veterans—as John Dornton had apparently done—was despicable. Thank God we've moved beyond that crap, I thought. Today a protester may trash the war, the President, and the entire US government, yet still show respect and decency toward the folks in uniform. Hell, some of my old college buddies protested against the Iraq War, but they'd never disrespect a veteran.

While I'd solved the mystery of why Dornton hated Archie, I hadn't found anything incriminating on Dornton, anything that might make him reconsider his uncompromising stance. The DA was determined to nail Archie to the wall, and there wasn't a hell of a lot I could do about it.

As things played out, Dornton didn't have to wait long. That night, as the strong eastern New Mexico wind blew tumbleweeds and the smell of manure across Maplefield, Archie's prostitute was back at work in front of the abandoned video store, her face clearly identifiable in the surveillance camera footage. I sent two of my officers to pick her up and bring her to the station for questioning.

Adela Moreno was her name, and Archie had been right about her. She was beautiful, with a look of youth and innocence that belied her profession. "Am I under arrest?" she asked with a Spanish accent.

"No, Ms. Moreno, you're not," I replied. "But I do have some questions for you."

She sat silently for a few seconds, and then said, "I want a lawyer. I won't answer any questions until I talk to a lawyer."

"Very well." I couldn't fault her for insisting on having an attorney. Though she hadn't yet been charged with a crime, she had to know she was in trouble. I excused myself and walked down the hall to the breakroom, where Dornton was waiting. (He had driven to the station immediately upon receiving my text informing him that Adela Moreno had been picked up. With his laptop in hand, he'd commandeered our breakroom and turned it into his own temporary office). When I told Dornton that Ms. Moreno insisted on having a lawyer present, he kicked one of the vending machines and chewed through a few of his favorite cuss words.

"I've got a proposal, Mr. Dornton," I said softly, trying to calm him down. "We've given this girl a good scare. How about we let her go, but tell her that if we ever catch her prostituting herself anywhere within the city limits, we'll bust her on the spot. Meanwhile, we give a similar warning to Archie—let him know that he's damn lucky to get off free this time, but he sure as hell better not solicit hookers again if he wants to stay out of jail. Then, we keep an eye on things, and see how they go. What do you think?"

I might as well have been talking to the vending machine he'd just kicked. After a dropping a few more f-bombs, Dornton gave me clear instructions: arrest the girl, get her a Public Defender, and work on a plea deal for her to testify against Archie. The bastard had it all figured out.

Over the following couple weeks, events unfolded just about the way Dornton wanted them to. We arrested Adela Moreno and got her a Public Defender, Chris Cutterfield, who arrived at the station within a half hour. Dornton worked on Cutterfield, advising him of the benefits that his client would obtain by cooperating as a witness against Archie. Cutterfield worked on the girl, and it wasn't a hard sell. I arrested Archie, which sucked. He handled things with stoic resignation. At first, he didn't even want a lawyer, but I insisted and he hired one—an old friend of mine with a solid reputation for integrity and fairness. But Archie chose not to mount an actual defense. He plead guilty.

Adela Moreno was convicted of prostitution but received a suspended sentence, the reward for her cooperation with Dornton's push against Archie. Surprisingly, she didn't reveal anything about a pimp or anyone else controlling her, even though we asked her repeatedly. Our surveillance cameras detected no more prostitution in the weeks that followed. The arrest of Adela had apparently scared the other hookers away.

Archie, in spite of his guilty plea, didn't fare well; he was sentenced to six months in prison—a pretty severe punishment for a "patronizing prostitutes" first offense.

After Archie began his prison sentence, Dornton seemed to relax. His demeanor in the office reflected a sense of satisfaction. And, as expected, he formally announced his campaign for the New Mexico State Senate. The incumbent Senator was retiring, and Dornton, having cultivated his image as the straight-shooter DA, quickly became the front-runner in the race to replace him.

I visited Archie several times in prison. I figured I owed it to him, considering all he'd done for the town and the crap deal he'd gotten. Generally, his attitude was upbeat; apparently, he'd adapted well to prison life. But he looked too damn skinny, and he seemed to lose more weight each time I saw him. He told me he was trying to put on some pounds, but some days he just couldn't stomach the prison chow.

Archie told me that a number of his friends, as well as former customers and employees from his garage, visited him regularly. I was pleasantly surprised to hear this, given the way we'd all neglected him in the months following his wife's death. His most notable visitor was Adela Moreno, who came several times over the course of his sentence. She wanted to visit him more often, but she'd apparently moved out of Maplefield to Lubbock, Texas, about 90 miles away. She came when she could.

As Archie explained during one of my later visits, Adela first came to the jail about two weeks into

130

his sentence, motivated by her feelings of guilt for having, in her view, contributed to his downfall. Almost immediately, a friendship developed. The two of them had chemistry—not in a romantic sense, but more in the sense of a father-daughter relationship. The girl was bright. She had recently landed a job at Walmart and started taking classes at an online university. As Archie had suspected, her foray into prostitution had been brief and coerced. Not willing to provide details, Archie strongly implied that Adela had either been trafficked or enticed into becoming a hooker. Whatever the case, he seemed relieved with the upward trend in the girl's fortunes. Yet he also worried about her.

Neither of Archie's sons bothered to visit him even once while he was in prison—not surprising, I suppose, but damn appalling.

By the time Archie completed his prison term and returned home, the town of Maplefield had finished dethroning him. Longwood Junior High had been renamed to Maplefield Junior High. Longwood Avenue had become Evans Avenue. All references to Archie, including an entire page containing his biography and pictures from his years in Vietnam, were purged from the town's website. Even his former business, Lion's Automotive, had become Maplefield Automotive. There would be no more limo rides in Independence Day parades or invitations to speak at Rotary Club dinners. Maplefield had washed itself clean of Archie Longwood. The Lion had fallen.

I visited Archie at home three days after his release from prison. He looked even thinner than he had the last time I'd seen him in jail a few weeks earlier, but he seemed to be in good spirits. We chatted briefly, and I promised to return a couple days later with one of my wife's homemade apple pies. "We'll put some weight on you, dammit," I said.

I returned two days later, fresh apple pie in hand, but there was no answer when I rang the doorbell. I was half expecting this; Archie hadn't answered my phone calls earlier that day. Perhaps he'd just gone out for a few hours, I figured.

But when Archie didn't answer my calls the following day, I knew something was wrong. I tried his cell phone and home phone repeatedly, with no luck. I called several of his friends; nobody knew where he'd gone. I would've called Adela Moreno, but she'd long since moved to Lubbock and we no longer had current contact information for her.

I figured the Lion's fate would be revealed soon enough, and I dreaded it. I remembered his Colt .45 pistol, sitting under the TV set. I wondered if Archie, saddened by the way the town had treated him and still grieving the loss of his wife, had killed himself.

On day three of Archie's absence, I filed a Missing Person report. With that report in hand and one of my officers in tow, I broke into Archie's house on a cool, autumn Saturday morning. As we kicked the door in, I half expected to be greeted with the stench of Archie's dead body. We found nothing—just the same cluttered house I'd seen a few days earlier. However, I did notice that his pistol was gone. This heightened my worry that he'd taken his own life. Maybe he'd gone off somewhere secluded to do it. How long would it take us to find him?

It didn't take long. On day five after Archie's disappearance, his older son, Frank, showed up at my office. Looking pale and distraught, he handed me an envelope containing a handwritten letter, from Archie, that he had received the previous day. In the letter, Archie explained where he had gone, why he had gone there, and what he planned to do.

Apparently, during his last month in prison, Archie's health had declined considerably. Looking downright emaciated, he was bedeviled by chronic fatigue and stomach pain. He concealed these symptoms from others. Maybe he didn't want to be a bother for anyone, or maybe he just didn't give a damn anymore. Finally, a week before his discharge, he was taken to the prison doctor for a full physical. The doctor was shocked at the state of Archie's health, and ordered the appropriate lab work. When the results of the tests came back, the day prior to Archie's departure from the jail, they were even worse than the doctor feared: Archie had an advanced case of stomach cancer.

The prison doctor forwarded the lab results to Archie's family physician and scheduled Archie for an appointment there, to occur the very day of his discharge from prison. But Archie missed that appointment.

When his doctor's office called him to reschedule, there was no answer.

During one of her visits to Archie in prison, Adela Moreno had told him about the man who'd pressured her into prostitution. Adolfo Del Rey, or "El Jefe" as he was sometimes called, had discovered Adela at a restaurant in the border city of El Paso, Texas, where she waited tables. Nineteen years old, beautiful, poor, from a broken home, she was just the type of girl he loved to prey upon. He started a romantic relationship with her. At first, he showered her with clothes, gifts, and attention. He promised even better things if she'd accompany him back to his hometown of Slatesville, Texas. He had business connections in Slatesville and nearby Maplefield, New Mexico, he told her, and he was an important man with lots of money. He loved her and wanted to provide for her.

Just as many other girls had likely done before, Adela fell for Adolfo's bullshit. She didn't know that Slatesville was a dumpy, flat town of only 10,000 people and that Maplefield wasn't much bigger. She didn't know that Adolfo was a sadistic con man. Under the spell of Adolfo's charms, she accompanied him to Slatesville.

Within hours of their arrival, her life changed dramatically. The gifts, flattery and affection were replaced by verbal abuse and the demand that she work as a prostitute. When she refused, she was beaten. When she refused again, she was locked in a room for two days with no food, water, or access to the bathroom. Finally, she gave in. She worked the streets of Slatesville, under Adolfo's supervision, for about a month. Then, she was driven to Maplefield and placed in a shabby apartment with two other girls. The three of them were watched constantly by a pair of Adolfo's pals, who brought them food and other supplies. By day, they hung around the apartment and slept. By night, they worked the streets. The quantity and quality of the food they ate depended upon the amount of business they did. If the girls got customers, they were fed well. If business was slow, they ate very little. Periodically, they were beaten—sometimes to punish them for not generating enough money, sometimes at random to remind them who was in charge.

A couple months after Adela's arrival in Maplefield, on that cool, March Saturday night, Archie had his fateful encounter with her.

Soon after Archie and Adela's trials were over, Adela made her escape to Lubbock, where she got help from social services and rented a small apartment. Within a couple weeks, she had her job at Walmart, was taking classes online, and felt hopeful for the first time in months. But she didn't feel safe. Adolfo was still out there, somewhere. Adela had avoided telling us about him when she was questioned, apparently out of fear. Now that she was on her own, she felt a gnawing terror that Adolfo might decide he'd be better off with Adela dead, lest she ever squeal on him.

Arriving home from prison, Archie knew he'd probably die within months, regardless of what he did. Deeply concerned about Adela's safety, Archie, whose courage and compassion had saved the lives of other Marines in the jungles of Vietnam, decided to save one more life before he lost his own. Realizing that the prick DA, Dornton, would have little interest in pursuing a case against Adolfo Del Rey—especially as a favor to

Archie—he must've concluded that in this situation, the moral law trumped the statutory law.

Archie didn't tell Adela what he planned to do; he knew she wouldn't have approved. He didn't want her to worry about him, either. Most importantly, he didn't want her, or other girls, to continue to live in fear of Adolfo. So, he acted quietly. Using the information Adela had provided him, plus the fruits of his own research, he traveled to Slatesville, Texas, carrying his notebook and his Colt .45.

The letter that Archie sent, postmarked from Slatesville, didn't tell us how the story ended. Frank Longwood and I got in my squad car and headed down there, where we spoke with the local police chief and several eyewitnesses. From these interviews and the information in Archie's letter, we put together a pretty clear picture of how things went down.

Apparently, it took Archie less than a day to find Adolfo in Slatesville. Surrounded by his fellow thugs in a local strip club, downing shots of tequila while several strippers—perhaps girls in his employ, other victims of his charms—danced in thongs and high heels, Adolfo must've been surprised by the bearded, cadaverous gringo who entered the club and approached him so directly. By the time "El Jefe" or his pals could react, Archie, only a few feet away, had drawn his weapon and pointed it straight at the animal's chest. Adolfo's henchmen were quick to deploy their own firepower; they felled the Lion in a wave of bullets. But they weren't quick enough. Before going down, Archie pumped three rounds into Adolfo, two of which struck the beast's heart. The bastard never had a chance—and neither did Archie.

By the time the local police arrived at the bar, Adolfo's thugs had gotten out of there, carrying the bodies of Adolfo and Archie, leaving a bloody trail behind them. One can hardly imagine the scene—blood, death, confusion, and the screaming and wailing of the strippers. Adolfo's henchmen dumped both bodies into a local lake before beating it out of town and heading southeast on Route 84.

The Slatesville police sent an all-points bulletin to state and local police departments in Texas. Meanwhile, the thugs got onto Route 385 at Littlefield and worked their way south toward Odessa. I suppose they were hoping to make it to the Mexican border.

In the outskirts of Odessa, nearly five hours after leaving Slatesville, the criminals found themselves being tailed by a pair of squad cars. A brief chase ensued, ending in an ugly accident that killed two of the four punks and left the other two hospitalized for several days. When they left the hospital, they were charged by Texas authorities with reckless driving, resisting arrest, assault, the possession of narcotics (the result of a stash of crystal meth found in the car), and murder. In addition, they faced extradition to New Mexico to face charges of promotion of prostitution, kidnapping, assault, and human trafficking. They'll spend the rest of their lives in jail.

Our trip to Slatesville was like a kick to the gut. We learned that Archie's body had been discovered in the lake and transported to the local morgue, along with that of Adolfo Del Rey. Having no identification on his person, his face somewhat disfigured from a gunshot wound, Archie had been a mystery to the Slatesville police. Fortunately, Frank was able to make a positive identification. It killed me to watch the poor guy's face when the mortician lifted the sheet to reveal what was left of his father. As the tears flowed from his eyes, I wondered how much remorse Frank must've felt for being so cold to his dad all those years.

We brought Archie back to Maplefield, and his funeral was held several days later. A substantial crowd, including two former mayors, the pastors of several churches, most of Maplefield's small business owners, and scores of ordinary folks who'd known Archie over the years, attended. All of the current political bigwigs stayed away. I figured they didn't want to appear to endorse Archie's vigilante actions, which was understandable. And of course, Dornton was nowhere in sight.

Despite the steady breeze that day, the air smelled fresh and clean. After we pallbearers had set Archie's casket down at the front of the church and taken our seats, I noticed Adela Moreno, seated in the back row, clad in a black dress, her face covered in a black veil. I nodded at her, and she nodded back, but I never got a chance to chat with her. She left immediately after the service concluded.

Following the funeral, Frank Longwood began the task of dispensing Archie's estate. Designated the executor of Archie's will, he accepted my assistance, which I offered eagerly. He was disappointed, even a bit angry, when he discovered that Archie had changed the will during his time in prison. Instead of dividing up his assets 50/50 between the two sons, the assets were divided 33/33/33, with Adela Moreno getting an equal share as Frank and Rex. Maybe Archie thought of Adela as the daughter he never had. During his months in prison, she'd certainly shown more devotion to him than his sons had.

In a desperate situation in 1965, Sergeant Archie Longwood risked his life to save the lives of his fellow Marines. Yet he always eschewed the "hero" label, insisting that he'd just been doing his duty. Likewise, fifty years later, when he walked into a filthy bar to confront a monster, he must've felt he was just doing his duty. Certainly, the law could never condone the vigilante justice that Archie had inflicted upon Adolfo

Del Rey. But I suspect that, for young women like Adela Moreno and others who'd shared her misfortune, Archie's actions have brought some measure of peace. And a significant, but ultimately unknowable, number of young women—poor, vulnerable girls in El Paso and other Texas towns—will live happier lives as a result of Archie's actions.

In the weeks following Archie's death, Dornton's behavior became downright disgusting. He seemed to gloat whenever Archie's name was mentioned. "Shame," I once overheard him say, "Shame that old bastard, after being treated like a hero, turned out to be a common criminal and a killer. Such a shame."

Eventually, Dornton became intolerable, and I decided I couldn't accept the idea of him being rewarded for his cruelty by getting elected to the State Senate. An asshole like Dornton—ruthless, self-serving and devoid of a conscience—had to be stopped.

So, a couple weeks after Archie's funeral, I retired from the police department and submitted my name as a candidate for the open State Senate seat.

Though new to politics, I had plenty of well-connected friends. I campaigned my ass off, and I never missed an opportunity to tell the voters exactly what I thought of Dornton and what he'd done to Archie. In the end, I won the election with 68 percent of the vote. Soon afterward, Dornton resigned as DA and left town. Some say he moved to Houston, Texas, where he has extended family, but nobody knows for sure. Nobody cares.

One of my goals as a newly minted politician is to revive, and render proper respect to, the legacy of Archie Longwood. I realize that schools and streets will never again be named in his honor. Nonetheless, his extraordinary service in uniform and his many contributions to our community should be given their proper due in the lore of Maplefield. All things considered, I figure that's the least I can do for my old friend, the Lion.

Made in the USA
Middletown, DE
24 December 2024